Raven Creek

Raven Creek

THERESE PAUTZ

ISBNs:
978-0-9885605-2-9 (pbk)
978-0-9885605-3-6 (ebk)
Library of Congress Catalog Number: 2021911653

Front cover artwork: Bur_malin/Shutterstock.com (sunset); © MARCEL/ Stocksy United (bird)
Cover and book design by Mayfly Design

First Printing: 2021
Printed in the United States of America

To my husband, David Graham, with love.

One

I KILLED MY DAD. Unlike past dreams, I wake without tears or remorse.

"Bridget, you're going to be late for school," Mom hollers up the stairs.

I push aside the lumpy, plum-colored comforter and sit on the edge of the double bed I share with my four-year-old sister, Zinnia. Her thumb is halfway in her mouth. Blonde ringlets frame her round face. She's clutching Mr. Hoppy, a well-loved bunny I gave her for her first birthday.

Twelve years older, I look nothing like Zinnia who resembles Mom: fair-skinned, petite, blonde, and pretty. I, on the other hand, have long, straight, mousy brown hair, which I mostly keep in a ponytail, and squinty hazel eyes with barely noticeable eyelashes. My nose isn't a cute button nose. It's long and broad. These features on Dad are rugged, maybe even handsome, but on me they're plain awkward.

A branch thuds against the bedroom window of the small, two-story stucco house we rent in Raven Creek, a God forsaken town in northern Minnesota, which has only one stoplight that everyone blows through and is four hours away from everyone I've ever known.

After Dad announced he had a new job opportunity in Raven Creek, I begged to stay in Minneapolis and live with Grandma Rita, Mom's mother. Dad said that would happen over his dead body. Their hatred is mutual. There was no arguing: I would not be returning to my old high school and Emma, my best friend, who knows things I never told anyone else and who likes to hang out, draw, and watch Harry Potter movies.

I get out of bed and pull aside the sheet covering the bedroom's single window. It overlooks a yard enclosed with a rusty chain-link fence. A towering oak tree releases dull brown leaves. The late September sky is dark and threatens rain.

Mom is wearing a floor-length pink fluffy robe and cooking bacon in the kitchen. Her wavy blonde hair falls untamed to her shoulders. There's a rat's nest on the back of her head. She studies my outfit. "Don't you have anything else?"

I'm wearing the sweatshirt that Emma gave me the night before we left Minneapolis. Emma wrote by the back tag with a permanent marker: "Friends no matter what. Love you!" I don't wash it because you can't always trust that permanent means permanent.

I retrieve the nearly empty box of Froot Loops from the cabinet and skim milk from the refrigerator and slump into a chair at the round wood table. I pour the last loops, including the dusty bits, into the plastic bowl. The milk doesn't change the cereal's staleness. As I eat, my finger finds the emerging zit on my forehead. I know I shouldn't touch it, but I can't help myself.

Dad bursts into the kitchen reeking of cheap cologne. He's wearing a slightly wrinkled white dress shirt with jeans. His dark hair is slicked back. Stubble shadows his square jaw.

He cups Mom's butt. "Ah, the queen and the princess." He pulls aside her hair and kisses the red hickey.

Mom playfully pushes him away. "Do you want two fried eggs and toast with bacon?"

Dad strides to the chair opposite me. "No time for that.

I got busy with other things this morning, remember?" He winks at Mom and thrusts his feet into the scuffed black shoes.

Mom frowns and turns off the burner. "When will you be home to pick up Zinnia and me for Bridget's volleyball game?"

"Change of plans. I'm meeting someone after work to discuss a new business opportunity."

"She's starting tonight."

"There'll be other games." He tweaks my ponytail. "Right, kiddo?"

I wince. Thick rain splats the window. Glancing at the clock on the stove, I say to Mom, "I need to FaceTime Emma before she catches the bus for school. Where's your phone?"

Mom avoids my eyes as she drains the bacon grease from the cast iron skillet into a chipped coffee mug. "You don't need to call her."

"But we talk every day."

Dad leans forward. His thick fingers grip my chin. He levels his eyes to mine.

"Carter," Mom pleads, "she's missing home and her friend."

"This is your home now," he says. "Got it?"

I know the look. And, I know not to look away.

A smile curls on Dad's lips when he finally releases my chin. The heat from his hands remains. I clamp my jaw shut, plunge the last bloated loop into the milk and study the small cuts in the oak table.

Dad slams the door on his way out.

"Don't be late for school," Mom says softly, squeezing my shoulder. She retreats upstairs. The bacon remains untouched.

When I go to dump the milk from my bowl into the garbage disposal, I see Mom's iPhone partially hidden by a dish towel. The screen is smashed. It looks like mine after Dad hit it with a hammer a week after Grandma Rita gave it to me for my 16th birthday.

Two

RAVEN CREEK HIGH SCHOOL stands two stories high with cement walls and narrow windows overlooking an asphalt parking lot filled with mostly pickup trucks. My old high school had floor-to-ceiling windows overlooking the Mississippi River and its tree-lined banks.

There's a collective buzz inside as people cluster in front of narrow, metal lockers. A group of girls on the volleyball team throw back their uni-blonde hair and laugh near the drinking fountain. I pass them, head down.

"It's in the genes," Mom boasted when I made the volleyball team. She constantly reminds me that the University of Minnesota-Duluth recruited her to play volleyball. Unfortunately, my birth foiled those plans.

The warning bell rings and people scatter. I move toward the staircase for first hour AP English. My hair falls forward and I don't bother brushing it aside or putting it behind my ear. It's my invisibility cloak.

A group of thick necked, wide shouldered guys yell, swear and push each other near the concrete steps. My gaze lowers as I press my body against the wall, but then, suddenly, a stocky dude with a buzz cut crashes into me and I collapse in pain onto the floor. It feels like a nail has been driven into my kneecap. No one cares as they continue their shouting while mounting the stairs.

Footsteps approach. "You okay?" The guy crouching beside me has dark brown eyes and lashes and is almost perfect except his nose looks like it's been broken. "Dirk, who knocked into you, is an asshole. He can't keep his mouth shut and is always messing with the wrong guys."

He helps me stand, as I reposition the backpack and shift the weight from my throbbing knee.

Doors close as classes start. "You're the new girl." He doesn't seem in any particular hurry as he leans against the lockers in his camo hoodie. "Are there a lot of gangs in Minneapolis? Is that why you moved here?" He folds his muscular arms across his broad chest.

"Yeah, that's it," I say sarcastically. "No, my dad's friend offered him a job here."

"I went to the Mall of America once. That's a big ass place. You go there?"

"Sometimes."

"Are you going to the football game on Friday against those pricks in Bemidji?" He tilts back the blaze orange baseball hat and says, like he's enticing me with a gooey dessert, "It'll be a good game."

"I can't. I've got things to do."

He smiles. "There's nothing to do in Raven Creek except go to the game."

I laugh. Not a cute laugh. It's high and fake, like a witch. I wish I could suck it back in.

"I hear you bumped Aimee Martin and are starting tonight."

I stare at my feet. "It's no big deal."

"She's pretty salty about it."

I want to scream: *I didn't even want to play on the stupid team!* I would have done a happy dance if I had been cut during tryouts, but I couldn't even do that right.

"She'll get over it." He says. "Or, she'll make your life miserable."

I don't know what's worse: my throbbing knee or my throat stuck in a vice grip. I'd rather crawl into a hole of rabid raccoons than stand here.

Footsteps approach. It's the principal's secretary, Mrs. Winkelman, who happens to be our neighbor. With her oversized, thick-lensed glasses, pasty skin and wiry silver hair, she looks like a snowy owl. Clearly, she's not happy we're lingering in the hall given her scowl and hastened waddle.

He raises his hand to fist bump. "I'm Brody Larson, by the way."

I pretend like I do this all the time even though it's apparent by my ill-timed response that I don't. "Bridget Reid."

Three

I DON'T TELL THE COACH OR TRAINER about my sore knee. Sitting alone on the wooden riser behind the team's bench, I flex and bend my knee as my stomach growls. There are no fans in the gym. As I reach into my duffle bag for the mini chocolate donuts, my too-perky teammate, Maddy, strides over and sits beside me.

"Do you have any idea how much sugar is in those? You'll be crashing mid-game."

"I'll keep that in mind."

"I have an extra apple. Want it?"

"No thanks, I'll live on the edge." I toss a donut in my mouth. Its fake chocolate coating is smooth and flavorless.

"You excited to start?" Maddy takes a big bite of a red apple.

I shrug.

"You've had really good games these past weeks. The coach likes you."

"Lucky me."

A group of teammates surround Aimee near the gym's entrance. Aimee's shiny black hair is parted down the middle. High cheekbones border a strong, wide nose. Her deep brown eyes cast a dagger of disdain in my direction. A sneer passes her lips.

"Did you play traveling volleyball in the Twin Cities?"

I shake my head. "Just Varsity." I don't say that Dad wouldn't let me travel.

"Seems like you did."

Will she ever stop talking? She's like a battery operated doll.

I shove the remaining donuts into my duffle bag and stand. She does too. With wavy strawberry blonde hair skimming her bony shoulders, she looks like a wind gust could blow her over. I start stretching in a hyper focused way with my back turned away from her. Eventually, Maddy waves to someone who looks like an older version of herself and darts off.

Fans for both teams arrive. Mom and Zinnia sit in the parents' section, but higher up in the bleachers near the corner. Zinnia plays with my old Polly Pocket dolls spread out on the riser in front of her. Mom enthusiastically waves when I glance their way.

The warm-up time on the scoreboard counts down and the buzzer sounds. Each team huddles on the sidelines. Coach Anhorn reminds us to stay focused, play our own game, and keep our egos off the court. The cheerleaders offer lame inspiration while most of the student section remains glued to their phones. A few parents clap.

The team lines up as the announcer prepares to introduce the starters before the anthem. Aimee not so subtly jabs her elbow into my side as she passes the spot she once occupied. When I hear my name, I step out and give the standard wave and forced smile. I hope it doesn't look too much like a parade wave.

Mom and Zinnia yell, "Go Bri!"

Brody sits wide legged in the student section on the front row of the bleachers with the other football players. He flashes me the thumbs up, and I can't help but smile.

My heart beats fast as the game starts. The cheering becomes loud and continuous. I forget about my knee. And Aimee. It's my best game ever.

All I can think about now is winning.

When it's my turn to serve for the match win, the crowd stands amid deafening cheering and stomping on the wood risers. I can barely breathe as I toss the ball up and hit it. It slams deep into the right corner. The six foot blonde on the other team dives, but misses the inbounds serve.

We've won!

The team rushes over and embraces me. Coach Anhorn offers uninspiring post-game comments and then the team scatters. Mom and Zinnia weave through the crowd. Zinnia jumps into my arms, almost tipping me backwards. She smells like popcorn and Skittles. Mom starts replaying the game. She's like that. For once, I'm okay with it.

My attention diverts. Brody and Aimee stand close together in the far corner of the gym. When she looks up at him, he lifts a strand of her straight hair and tucks it behind her ear. Then, he kisses her on the mouth, puts his arm around her waist and they leave together.

Mom studies my face. "What's wrong?"

"Nothing. My knee's bothering me."

Her expression turns to worry. "Has the trainer looked at it?"

"It'll be fine," I say. "I'll meet you outside."

Only a few people linger after Mom and Zinnia leave. The scoreboard is dark. A hunched janitor carries a large plastic garbage bag, combing the bleachers for trash.

I step over empty water and Gatorade bottles and pick up the volleyball. Tossing it in the air, I try to remember when everything felt right and I mattered. When the ball falls to the ground, I kick it across the gym.

"Dang, what did that ball ever do to you?"

Maddy strides across the gym with her hair free from

the game day ponytail. She's wearing skinny jeans, a belted jacket and black boots.

"You do remember that we won, right?" There's a hint of sweet, floral perfume as Maddy nears.

"I could have done better."

"Give me a break. The last serve was epic."

"It was lucky."

"I would have been happy to play. I think the coach hates me." Maddy waves to a lanky guy near the entrance. "We're going for pizza now. Wanna come?"

"My mom's outside waiting for me. Thanks though." I pick up my warmup jacket.

"Come on. Evan's driving and there's room for you too. We can drop you off afterwards. It won't be late."

I hesitate, which is a mistake because Maddy smiles and says, "Great. I'll meet you outside."

A blustery wind blows leaves across the cracked asphalt parking lot. Across the street, two ramblers compete for the tackiest Halloween lawn decorations. I shiver and pull my volleyball warmup jacket closer as I walk toward Mom's Ford Focus parked near the lamp post.

Mom lowers the driver's window as I approach. "Did the trainer look at your knee?"

"It's fine." As nonchalantly as I can, I add, "Maddy, my teammate, asked me to go out for pizza. She'll give me a ride home."

Maddy crosses the lot with Evan, a long-legged senior wearing a letter jacket. They're holding hands and dodging the puddles left after the day's steady rain.

"Please." I don't point out that I haven't asked to do anything with anyone since we moved here at the end of August. Not that anyone asked me. But, that's beside the point.

Mom glances at the clock on the dashboard. "Okay. But, don't stay out late." I can tell she's relieved that someone might want to be my friend.

She retrieves a wrinkled 20 dollar bill from her purse. She sneaks money from the stash Dad keeps under the top mattress of their bed. I tuck it into the front pocket of my warmup pants.

The car's rear door squeaks when I open it. I toss my backpack beside Zinnia who is buckled in the high-backed booster seat and sucking her thumb. Her heavily lashed eyes open slightly. I blow a kiss, which she catches in her fist before I shut the door.

Maddy waves. I give a quick, waist level wave back. Instantly, I cringe. How come I didn't lift my arm and wave like a normal person? I take a deep breath and start walking toward Maddy and Evan.

I don't get far.

A black Ford F-150 pickup truck with dealer plates squeals into the lot, angles across two spots, and parks next to Mom's car. Mud is splattered on the truck's fender. The driver's tinted window rolls down.

It's Dad.

There's a man sitting in the passenger seat. I can't see his face in the shadows. Then, he leans forward. A smile creeps below his narrow mustache. "You're sure as hell better looking than your old man."

Dad withdraws a cigarette from his mouth and tosses the butt to the ground as Mom comes to stand beside me.

The stranger laughs. "Now it makes sense."

"Shut up, Jags." Dad's voice slurs.

Inspecting the car, I mutter under my breath, "I thought we didn't have any money?"

Mom puts her hand on my arm to silence me. "Carter, you wouldn't believe the game that Bridget had."

A lopsided smile appears. "That's my girl. Kicking ass." He turns to Jags, his new friend. "Gets that from her old man. I was the star quarterback."

He doesn't mention he played only one season at community college because Mom surprised him with the news of my impending arrival. Reluctantly, he switched to the automotive training program at the technical college and relinquished his dreams of a college football career.

Maddy and Evan wait outside a white minivan. The wind gusts. I decide to try and make a quick exit, even though I know that my odds of joining them are now crap.

"I'll be back by ten," I say to Mom.

Dad scowls. "Where the hell you going?"

"It's only pizza."

Dad opens his door. "Pizza my ass. I gotta meet anyone you go out with."

"It's no big deal. They're on my team."

He staggers out and slams the truck door. "Since when do guys play volleyball?" His breath smells like whiskey and Altoids.

"Never mind." I lower my voice. "I don't need to go out."

I pray he doesn't make a scene in front of Maddy and Evan. My eyes plead for him to get back into the truck.

"Damn straight." Dad snakes his fingers through his thick, disheveled hair. "I can't have my daughter running loose around town and getting into trouble. It makes me look bad."

Jags smirks.

I motion for Maddy and Evan to go on without me.

Four

THE NEXT DAY I stop at "Val's Bait and Thrift," which I walk by every day on my way home from volleyball practice. I still have the 20 dollar bill that Mom gave me last night. Even if I had all the money in the world, I'd still thrift. People discard what they no longer want and I give them a home again. Dad hates it. He wouldn't be caught dead wearing someone else's clothes.

The wood sign hangs askew on two thick chains above the entrance. Bordering the bold yellow lettering are hand-painted pictures of a blue lake, pine trees and a hooked fish. A Chevy Trailblazer with the license plate "GottaBe" parks in front.

A bell announces my arrival. No one is in sight. The air inside is warm and smells fishy. New Age instrumental music plays softly. Three tanks of minnows and an upright refrigerator line one wall. There are shelves on another wall with maps of local lakes, Styrofoam buckets and fishing gear identified as: bobbers, line, hooks, jigs, sinkers, scoops, and tip-ups.

I stumble on the edge of a propane tank and fall toward the counter. Plastic containers full of little worms and sawdust begin spilling. I catch them before they hit the ground.

A woman with gray hair stacked high on her head struts through dangling, multi-colored glass beads. "That coulda been a helluva mess." There's a stud in her broad, hooked nose. Her fleshy arms are thick with tattoos.

"Sorry."

"No worries. It happens to more people than I can count."

I re-stack what I see now are "wax worm" packages. "You could move the tank out of the way."

The woman peers over her purple glasses. "Well, aren't you a smart thing."

"It's pretty tight in here."

"Top of my list is to get an interior designer in here to explore layout options. I'll let you know when it's scheduled so you can give your input."

My face feels hot. I look down.

"You come in here for any reason other than to give good old Val some business advice?" Her voice is husky.

"I thought you might have some clothes."

"You name it, we got it. Except maybe a good catch." She laughs deeply, then starts coughing. Grabbing a tissue from her full cleavage, she hacks something into the tissue. "You're not from around here, are you, child?"

"No. And, I'm *not* a child."

She laughs. "There's not a person your age who doesn't want to be all grown up. Shame that you have to be my age to start acting like a child."

"I'm looking for jeans if you have any."

"Follow me, sweet thing." Her wide butt sways like the beads as she leads me to the back room which is musty but larger than the overpacked bait shop. Unfolded clothes are piled on plastic rectangular tables.

"You'll have to dig."

I start lifting mostly old people clothes-a shirt here, a sweater there. I don't touch the pile of underwear.

"Do you have any little kids' clothes?"

"How old?"

"Four. A girl."

"Check the table near the far wall."

Val tosses items in my direction like they're radioactive. Most land on the cement floor. Digging through the clothes, I find a pair of jeans in my size and a pink sweatshirt with Elsa from *Frozen* on the front for Zinnia.

The bell announces a customer in the bait shop. Val leaves me alone, promising to be back soon.

I scan the room to see if there's anything I've missed. In the corner, there's a round card table with knick knacks, picture frames and books. I walk over to see if the books interest me, or if there are any art supplies.

There's an "I Love Paris" snow globe. It reminds me of Grandma Rita's collection. She has a table in a spare bedroom filled with them. When I was young, I spent hours studying the idyllic glass enclosed scenes. Some even played music. I shake this one and snow sparkles and floats over the Eiffel Tower.

Jamming the snow globe into my coat pocket, I go out front to pay.

Val looks up at me. "Find anything?"

I place the items on the counter. "Just these."

"I got coats that will actually keep you warm."

"I'm good."

Lines deepen on Val's leathered face as she narrows her dark eyes. "That thin coat is worthless."

Val retreats to the back room. Eventually, she returns. "I got this gem. It'll fit perfectly." She holds up a hooded North Face ski jacket. It looks new. There's not a tear or mark on its white surface.

I push the coat aside and hold out the 20. "I don't have enough money."

"You got plenty." She takes my money and jams the jacket into the bag and pushes it toward me.

The pirated snow globe weighs heavy in my pocket.

Val releases the hair mounted high on her full face and shakes it out. "What's your name?" She twists her hair into a braid with swift hands and secures it with a binder and bobby pins.

"Bridget Reid."

"Well, Bridget, you come back any time you need something or have more business advice you want to dole out. I'm always here." She retrieves a large handbag from behind the counter and digs until she retrieves a lipstick tube and compact mirror. "But, you need to get now. I've got a hot date."

Five

"IT'LL BE OUR SECRET." Mom says when I ask if I can sleepover at Maddy's. "Dad and Jags will not be back from Fargo until Sunday."

Maddy's split-level house sits on the outer end of town. A wall of thick pine trees separate their expansive front lawn from the neighboring, harvested field. Two snowmobiles park on the side of a three-car garage.

Maddy opens the front door as I approach. "I was beginning to think something came up or your mom changed her mind."

Her parents, introduced as Doug and MaryAnne, wave hello and say the pizza is on the way. Skipper, their thick coated, slow moving golden retriever follows us to the lower level. A leather sectional faces a flat screen TV spanning most of the knotty pine wall. Red vinyl covered stools line the bar. Behind it, there's a full-sized fridge and standing popcorn machine on wheels.

Skipper plops down on the couch and studies me with opaque eyes. He smells like dead leaves and mud.

Maddy hands me a Diet Coke. "I can't believe we didn't make it to State in volleyball. At least we have next year."

I pet Skipper's head. "Who knows if I'll be here."

"You wouldn't leave your senior year, would you?"

"Why not?"

"You'd miss graduating with your friends."

"We move a lot. I don't get too attached to any one place.

Not even one as nice as Raven Creek." By the look on Maddy's face, she doesn't pick up on the sarcasm.

The doorbell rings. "I'll be right back," Maddy says. She goes upstairs to get the pizza and, when she returns, Skipper's attentive, and ready for handouts.

Maddy nibbles pizza like a squirrel while I snarf it.

Freckles sprinkle her high cheekbones and narrow nose. I notice a hole in my sock and cover it with my other hand.

Maddy scans her phone for earth shattering news. She pauses and looks at me. "Can you believe Aimee and Brody broke up? Everyone thought they'd get married."

"Wow, I wonder if the world will continue to spin."

"You really don't like Aimee, do you?"

"What's to like?"

"She acts tough but she's gone through some heavy shit," Maddy says. "Her cousin went to work at the casino one day and never came back. It's like she disappeared."

I put the rest of the pizza slice I've been eating into the box. "I wouldn't mind if my dad left and never came back."

"Come on. You don't mean it."

Skipper rolls immodestly onto his back. I rub his belly and, for a moment, wonder if I should share more.

Maddy's phone dings.

"It's Evan," she says. "I gotta call him back."

She takes the rest of the pizza upstairs and I wander to the back wall. It's a dry erase painted surface covered with brightly colored drawings and comments. I can't believe Maddy's mom has spent much time gazing at the wall. Picking up a red marker, which smells like tart cherry, I begin drawing in the lower section where there's a small open space.

Maddy bounds down the stairs, tucking her phone into the front of her low hanging jeans. Her pelvic bones jut out, cradling her flat stomach and "outie" bellybutton.

"Evan's folks are gone. People are heading there for a bonfire. Want to snowmobile over?"

"Your parents okay with that?"

"They love Evan. As far as they know, he's a saint."

It's true. Maddy's parents don't bat an eye when she shares the plan. The only conditions, muttered with eyes glued to Fox News: wear helmets, stick to the trail that follows the county road, and return before midnight.

six

MADDY STEERS THE SNOWMOBILE down Evan's snow packed gravel driveway. There's a garage resembling a multi-unit storage building with a flat tin roof and an outside mounted light. The two-story farmhouse is dark. She parks among other snowmobiles and pickup trucks.

Maddy looks perfect when she removes her helmet. She struts toward the fire pit where people greet her enthusiastically. Flames flit through billowing smoke. I stand on the sidelines: the mute tag-a-long. Evan pulls her close. I watch out of the corner of my eye longer than I should. Then, when I'm even embarrassed by myself, I look up at the night sky. Stars, more numerous and brighter than I've ever seen, form constellations that I once learned about, but have long forgotten. I remove the stocking cap Maddy loaned me and coax limp hair off my face.

"Maddy said you might stop by." I turn and see Brody. "No drink yet?"

"I'm not thirsty."

"You can have mine, if you like."

"No, thanks."

Maddy puts her arms around Evan's neck. He tilts his head back playfully.

Brody holds out a can of beer. "Go on, it'll loosen you up."

I cross my arms over my chest. "Why would I want to be loose?"

He laughs, then walks toward the picnic table strewn with bags of opened Ruffles sour cream and onion chips, Twizzlers, and jerky. A cooler filled with beer and ice is propped open. Music blasts from mini speakers. I stop and lean against a thick oak tree outside the circle of people I've seen before, but never talked to. Brody motions me closer. Despite wanting to run in the opposite direction, I enter the space he's created for me.

Gradually, people start talking to me. They ask about my old school and laugh when I tell them I've never been in the Northwoods before, let alone on a snowmobile.

"All we got here is clean living," says Dirk, who bumped me to the ground at school, bruising my knee.

I take the beer Dirk hands me.

Words start flowing. When I tell them about the food fight that broke out in the high school cafeteria, I sound tough and almost believe what I'm spouting even though it didn't happen during my lunch period and I watched it on YouTube.

A dwindling group of us sit in plastic chairs scattered around the fire pit. I lose track of the number of beers I drink. My tongue thickens and my words jumble.

Embers smolder in the fire pit. I stagger to the picnic table through groups of people who now know my name. The food is gone. So are Maddy and Evan.

My breath lingers in the air. I grasp the table's corner as my body sways. I look down the long, dark driveway.

An arm wraps around my shoulder. "Hey, kiddo."

It's Dirk.

"I need to find Maddy."

He pulls me in. "I can give you a ride."

"She was just here."

He grabs my arm. "I'll help you." Stubble scratches my cheek.

I yank my arm free. "I need to find Maddy."

"That's my Chevy Impala right there. Helluva lot warmer than standing outside."

I can't think. Or breathe. The ground teeters.

"Hey, bro," says Brody, striding toward us. He slaps Dirk on the shoulder. "I thought you were leaving."

Dirk scowls. "Why would I be doing that?"

"Because it'd be a good idea," Brody says, "before you get yourself in trouble."

"I ain't doing nothing."

"That's right. You're not."

"Fuck off," Dirk growls.

Brody steers me away. "I'm giving you a ride home. Maddy's gone off with Evan. You can't stay here. Not like this and not with him."

Dirk flips Brody the finger and mutters something under his breath.

My feet stumble on the uneven ground. Brody guides me down the driveway. He lifts me up and into the front seat of his pickup truck. The door slams. I lean my face on the cold glass and close my eyes. Everything spins. When I taste vomit rising in my mouth, I struggle and fail to open the door. The vomit goes all over my lap and the front seat of the truck.

Brody's voice sounds distant and muted as everything goes dark.

Seven

I WAKE UP SHIRTLESS in a place I don't recognize. With only my bra and pants on, I'm lying on a soft, moss colored pull-out couch overlooking a snow covered lake lined with pine trees. There are no houses in sight, only an emerging pale pink sunrise. A patchwork quilt covers me.

My dry mouth tastes foul and my head pounds. There's a glass of water on a cork coaster and an Advil bottle within reach on the square coffee table with engrained, concentric circles. I swallow three tablets and guzzle the tepid water. My mind swirls. The last thing I remember is standing around the fire pit. I pull the quilt closer. It smells sweet, like cinnamon rolls. My stomach feels sick.

Where's Maddy?

A toilet flushes. Val emerges in the arched doorway dressed in a red poppy kimono barely reaching shiny purple slippers.

"Look who's awake bright and early."

I sit up, clutching the quilt. "Why am I here?" My voice croaks and feels scratchy.

"Brody brought you." Her hair falls wild. "After you puked in his truck and passed out, he had to bring you somewhere. He didn't know where you lived."

"He's your son?"

"Oh, hell, no. I was smart enough not to marry his dad. But, I'm the best mother he almost had."

"My mom is going to kill me," I groan. "I was supposed to sleep at Maddy's."

"Maddy Daniels ditched you?"

"You know her?"

"Honey, I know everyone." She laughs, then adds a quick wink. "Except a good man."

Val walks toward the adjacent kitchen.

Maybe I can sneak in before Mom wakes up and Dad gets home from Fargo. Oh God, what if Maddy's folks are looking for me? Mom will be freaking out. She maybe even called Dad already.

"I have to get home," I say.

"After you eat."

"I can't eat."

"A little grease soothes the gut after too much booze."

"I can walk if you just tell me the way."

"That would take some time and you'll get frostbite with the temperatures dipping below zero. No, I'll take you after I get some coffee in me. And, food in you."

"But . . ."

Val plants her hands on her broad hips. "You're not going anywhere until I get things moving inside. That takes time in the morning. We'll go soon enough." Her raised eyebrow and piercing stare say the discussion, if you could call it that, is over. She turns toward the avocado colored fridge. After retrieving bacon and eggs from it, she heaves two cast iron frying pans from the drawer beneath the white stove. I wince at the banging.

Val waves silver tongs at me. "I need to get you something to wear other than the quilt my mama made me." She disappears down a short hallway.

The sun brightens the sky. A large yard leads to the lake

with at least half a dozen bird feeders of varying sizes. A bright red cardinal perches on the one closest to the window.

Val returns and hands me a black t-shirt with the word, "Resist." She doesn't direct me to the bathroom or anywhere else to put it on. She simply turns her back. I drop the quilt and lift the soft, oversized shirt over my head. The hole in my sock has grown, exposing a jagged big toenail.

Val hums as the bacon sizzles. It's guttural and rhythmic. The greasy smell turns my stomach. I take deep breaths to avoid gagging.

"Make yourself useful. Set the table. OJ's in the fridge."

There are no cabinet doors. The plates, bowls, glasses, mugs, spices and other baking goods are exposed. Everything seems on the verge of falling out. I place plates and small juice glasses on the table. As I go to retrieve the OJ, I pause to look at the photographs plastering the fridge. Most of the people, young and old, are grinning and thrusting forward large, wide-mouthed fish. Disgusting. Why not pictures of cute puppies or kittens?

Val sets a platter of bacon, scrambled eggs and thick buttered toast on the table and sits next to me with a mug of black coffee. "Eat."

There's no use protesting. I take a small spoonful of eggs and a slice of bacon. As I nibble the greasy, undercooked bacon, I struggle keeping it down.

"Mrs. Winkelman tells me your family lives next door." My face must reveal my confusion because she explains, "She goes to my church. I put two and two together when you came into my store. How'd the clothes work out?"

"Fine." I stare at the eggs cut into miniscule pieces.

"That's good." Deep lines edge her mouth and wide-set eyes. "Did your sister like the snow globe?"

I look down. A sour taste rises and my stomach flips. I cover my mouth, willing the food to stay down.

Val pushes her chair back, lifts me by my arm and brings me to the sink. I bend over it, and the small bits of food I ate come up, followed by dry heaves. Val places a damp wash cloth on my forehead. She holds it in place until I'm done. Then, she wraps her massive, soft arms around my shoulders and steers me to the couch.

We sit together looking at the frozen lake. The sun shines bright in the cloudless, blue sky. I feel drained, but my head isn't pounding anymore and my stomach has calmed.

"I'm sorry for everything," I say. "I shouldn't have taken the snow globe. I can bring it back."

"Keep it. But, let's be clear: if we're going to be friends, and I think we are, you tell me what you need or want." There is no smile or levity in her expression or tone. "You just play it straight with old Val or there'll be hell to pay."

Eight

THERE TURNED OUT TO BE no viable excuse to stay home from school on Monday despite the multitude of proffered options. Without a fever or vomiting, I was doomed to show my face among people I may have met at the party.

I slink inside the school with my backpack weighing heavy on my shoulders while avoiding eye contact with any other mortals. Before I even see her, I hear Maddy's voice calling my name. I forge toward my locker.

Maddy catches up and says, breathlessly, "I'm sorry about Saturday night."

The padlock on my locker fails to open. I redial it without looking at Maddy.

"Evan and I went into the house to talk and fell asleep. When I woke up, everyone was gone."

The padlock releases. I grab the thick, three-ring binder from the top shelf, thrust the white North Face jacket inside, slam the metal door shut, and spin the padlock's numbers.

Maddy blocks my escape. "Don't be pissed."

Our eyes meet. "Did you ever wonder how I got home?"

"I knew you were okay because when I woke up I saw Brody's text that he was bringing you home."

"It never dawned on you to actually check to see if I was okay?"

Maddy brushes aside a strand of hair freed from her French braid. "How am I supposed to do that if you don't have a phone and haven't told me where you live?"

She had me there.

Brody walks through the main doors and joins his friends near the staircase. I probably watch him too long because Maddy's eyes widen. "Did something happen between you too?"

I scoff. Maddy blocks me when I try passing her. "Did it?" Her intense glare demands an answer.

I shrug. "Besides Brody professing his deep love and affection for me?"

Maddy's jaw drops. "Really?"

"Oh, and we couldn't keep our hands off each other. Besides that, totally uneventful."

"No. Way."

I burst out laughing.

Maddy hits my forearm. "Stop it. Seriously. You'd tell me if he did, wouldn't you? I mean, I'm practically your best friend."

"I don't exactly have people fighting for that title, you know. And, I'd be the last person Brody, or anyone else, would be interested in."

Maddy shakes her manicured finger at me. "Not true. Evan heard Dirk was hitting on you." In an effort to prod my recollection, she says, "Dirk Rasmussen. Thick neck, buzz cut. Loud. A wrestler. Ring a bell?"

"Oh, him," I say tentatively, trying to remember details through the fog of the night. "I think he gave me a beer." Maybe a lot more than one.

Brody approaches.

Maddy whispers, "I'll let you love birds talk in private."

She takes off while I look down and begin fumbling again with the combination, pretending I've forgotten something important and don't notice him approaching.

"Hey there."

I look up. Brody's not wearing a baseball cap. Soft brown hair curls over his cute, well-proportioned ears.

"Oh, hi."

"You doing okay?"

"Yeah, I just can't get this thing to click."

"Want some help?"

"I got it, thanks."

"Looks like you're having some trouble."

I kick the locker. "It's just stuck."

"Then definitely kick the hell out of it."

The warning bell rings.

I abandon my feigned efforts to open my locker. "I'm sorry about your truck. I feel terrible about that. I'm not much of a drinker."

"No shit." He smiles, exposing a deep dimple in his right cheek. "There's another party this Friday out at Pete Johnson's farm near the rez. I can pick you up in my newly cleaned truck if you want."

"I don't think so."

"Come on. You'll have fun."

"It's not that."

"You don't have to drink."

"I know."

"You have other plans?"

"Yah, that's it," I say, looking at him. "I have so many offers and this is the least attractive one."

"If you don't want to go, just say so."

"Sorry. No, it's my Dad. He's not much into me going places with guys."

"Dads, and I'm not even exaggerating, love me. Just like puppies, who also love me."

I can't help but smile. "Puppies love everyone."

"True, but they especially love me." He takes a step closer, resting his hand on my locker.

I duck under his arm and shake my head. "I can't risk it."

"So, you're like a doomed, forgotten princess locked away in a tower?"

I laugh. "He's not that bad, just overprotective. Daddy's little girl." I almost choke over that last bit.

"Dang," he says. "That sucks."

Astute and good-looking. And, he's actually wanting to see me again after I barfed in his truck.

I shouldn't, but I say, tentatively, "I could maybe sneak out after he goes to sleep." Or passes out.

"That works. Text me."

"Small problem. Did I mention he also doesn't let me have a phone?"

Brody looks like he was told aliens had invaded Raven Creek. "Are you Amish?"

"No," I say, "Just trapped in my own personal snow globe."

He laughs. I don't.

Brody opens his binder, tears out a piece of paper and writes on it. "Here's my number if you find a way to call from your mom's phone or, well, whatever, even use smoke signals."

I take it and stare at the number.

"You know," Brody says, "you could write down your address and tear it off and give it to me. That's kinda how this works, if we're going old school."

"Oh, right." I fumble trying to find a pen or pencil in my backpack, but there's only spiral notebooks, textbooks, graded assignments, and empty Snickers' wrappers.

He finally hands me his mechanical pencil and I scribble the address.

Nine

THICK SNOWFLAKES FALL OUTSIDE my bedroom window as I lay in bed waiting to meet Brody. I shake the stolen snow globe and watch the sparkly white flakes floating onto the golden Eiffel Tower.

I've replayed Monday morning's conversation countless times. No one has ever asked me out on a date. I considered confiding in Maddy, but I couldn't risk her talking to Brody and confirming I imagined it. Maybe he's this way with everyone? Still, I have the piece of paper with his number as proof. But, proof of what? I could crumple the paper, swallow it, and remember each number by heart.

Time crawls. Zinnia has been asleep next to me since half past ten. She lies sprawled sideways with the comforter kicked off despite the drafty room.

I glance at the photograph Zinnia retrieved from an unpacked box while digging for books she wanted me to read to her tonight. It was taken when I was eight years old. Mom, Dad and I were at the Corn Palace in Mitchell, South Dakota on our way to Mount Rushmore. A flowered scarf holds back Mom's sun bleached, shoulder-length hair. She's smiling as her arms engulf me. Dad leans on the truck and smokes. When the man who took the picture said Mom looked like a movie star, Dad threw down the cigarette, stamped it out and yanked Mom and me by the arm toward the truck. This ended our first, and only, family vacation.

Wind rattles the window. There is no moon visible. A tree

branch rhythmically scrapes the stucco. There hasn't been any recent ranting by Dad at the Minnesota Wild hockey game on TV or any footsteps back and forth to the kitchen. No one has come upstairs to check on us.

The bed groans as I stand, but Zinnia doesn't stir. I carry my shoes and creep down the bare stairs in my socks, sliding my hands on the thick wooden banister. Some steps creak unpredictably. Midway down, I pause and peer into the living room. The only light comes from the TV mounted on the wall to the side of the arched doorway. From the sounds of it, the hockey game is in the final minutes. Carefully I continue my descent.

I conceal my shoes near the front door and tiptoe into the living room.

Dad snores in the scuffed La-Z-Boy recliner. He's wearing a short sleeved t-shirt and jeans. There's a Jim Beam bottle and an empty glass on the floor. Mom's new iPhone is on the coffee table in front of the couch where she sleeps prone.

I cross the room as quietly as I can and lift Mom's phone like a surgeon extracting an organ during transplant surgery. Mom moans. I freeze. The phone is suspended in midair, ready to slip from my hand. When Mom rolls onto her side facing me, I expect her to open her eyes. I hold my breath. When her face relaxes and her breathing deepens, I cautiously move toward the front door.

Cold winter air seeps under the muddy brown door where, in the lower corner, are deep scratch marks, probably from a large dog. There is a small rectangular window near the top. All I can see is glistening, falling snow captured in the streetlight's beam.

My fast breath sounds loud in my head. I close my eyes and see Brody's number. Swallowing hard, trying to moisten my dry mouth, I call him.

He answers, too loud, on the first ring.

I whisper, "You can come by now."

"I'm already parked down the street."

I want nothing more than to skip, laugh out loud, and twirl, but I carefully creep back into the living room to return Mom's phone before sneaking out.

Ten

WARM AIR GREETS ME when I open the truck's door. A green pine scented piece of cardboard dangles from the mirror. I climb inside and buckle my seatbelt with a quick sideways look at Brody. He smiles, puts the truck in gear and starts driving.

The houses we pass are variations of each other: a mix of ramblers and small, two-story houses with detached garages. Power lines attach to wooden poles with outstretched arms and affixed lights.

I stare ahead like a zombie. I try to think of something to say. Nothing comes to mind. It's as if I've had a lobotomy. He's probably wondering why he even bothered to pick me up when he could be listening to sports radio or music just fine by himself. Maybe he's going to say this was a big mistake and offer to take me back home. Maybe he and Aimee got back together and he didn't know how to tell me?

For God's sake, I have to think of something interesting to talk about. My palms sweat.

Finally, I say, "It's cold out."

"It thickens the ice on the lake." I stare at him blankly. He explains, "For ice fishing."

What am I supposed to do with this information?

"Besides hunting and regular fishing, it's my favorite thing to do. Drill the hole with the auger, then sit and wait for the fish. Nothing better than pan-fried gills, perch or crappies through the ice."

Disgust contorts my face.

"Don't you like it?"

"Can't say I've ever had the delicacy."

"You should."

Brody pulls into the plowed lot of Raven Lake in the center of town. Structures of varying sizes dot the frozen lake.

"My icehouse isn't too far from shore if you want to check it out."

"Sure," I say, hesitantly.

He shifts into four-wheel drive and begins driving on the snow-covered ice. I grab the armrest and hold on tightly while questioning the sanity of the action. We don't drive far before stopping in front of a wooden structure that barely looks large enough for two people. The exterior is painted purple; the trim is canary yellow. A Minnesota Viking's pennant is tacked above the door.

Brody pushes the door open and I follow him inside. The floor is unpainted wood. He turns on a lantern strung from the ceiling. I can see my breath. The room smells like dead fish and propane. There are two holes drilled through the ice near the wall.

Brody turns on a portable space heater and cracks the window about an inch. He opens the cooler. "Busch Latte?" He hands me a beer. I open it and take a sip. He cracks another open and takes a long gulp. He sits in a chair, so I do too. Cold creeps through my jeans. He picks up a plastic container with multi-colored jigs (which he explains you need to catch fish) and takes out a chartreuse one with a hook and attaches it to clear line on a short pole. He pulls a plastic container of wax worms from his coat pocket and attaches one to the hook, then lowers it into the water after breaking the icy layer.

We stare into the dark hole. I'm not sure what is going to happen, but I feign interest.

Finally, Brody says, "We can go to Pete's party anytime you want. I thought you might want to experience ice fishing. And, it doesn't sound like too many people are there yet."

"This is fine," I say. "You come out here a lot?"

"As much as I can."

"You don't get bored?"

"Nope."

Who wouldn't want to freeze their butt off while staring into an abyss?

He holds up his empty can. "Another?"

"I'm good."

Ice augers groan outside. My feet feel like bricks of ice in my knock-off UGGs and my fingers feel like frozen sausages. I blow on my white knuckles.

Brody pulls out a brown round tin of chewing tobacco from his other back jean pocket. "Want some?"

"Don't tempt me."

An eternity passes silently.

Brody's phone buzzes. He retrieves it from his back pocket, and answers it. His face scowls. "Who the fuck are *you*?" He hangs up. The phone rings again. He answers it. "What the hell are you talking about. I don't know any Ashley."

Oh God.

My hands start shaking.

"I'd like to see you try." Brody hangs up the phone. "Freak."

My legs feel wobbly when I stand. "I have to go."

"Why?"

"I need to get home."

He looks baffled.

"That's my dad."

"Ashley?"

The confusion is evident on his face.

"My mom." My breath can barely escape my closed throat. "My dad must have looked at her phone and seen your number. We have to go. Now."

Eleven

THE SQUAD CAR'S BLUE AND RED LIGHTS flash silently in front of our house. Brody's truck is barely stopped when I thrust the door open and sprint toward the front door.

I don't make it far. Two officers emerge gripping Dad's arms, handcuffed behind his back. His thick black hair is disheveled. Blood soaks his white t-shirt.

I stop cold. Dad's expressionless and unapologetic eyes meet mine. A burly officer yanks him toward the squad car, pushes his head down and forces him into the rear seat. The door slams shut.

I bound the crumbling cement steps, burst inside and call for Mom. There's no answer.

The downstairs is lit up. Broken glass covers the floor. There are large shards from the wood framed oval mirror that hung on the wall above the couch and tiny fragments of blue, gold, green and red glass from the Tiffany style lamp, a wedding gift from Mom's parents that sat on the end table. I look down and see more blood splattered on the worn hardwood floor.

No sign of Mom.

The kitchen door swings open. An officer with a craggy face and a bushy white mustache and matching mop of hair, enters. He scowls when he sees me. "You can't be here."

"Where's my mom?" The question squeaks out, barely audible. "Zinnia?"

His expression softens. "Your mom's on the way to the hospital," he says. "A neighbor called 911. We got here as soon as we could." He doesn't say it's not serious, or she'll be okay, or don't worry.

"Zinnia?"

My body starts shaking. I wipe tears and snot with the coat's sleeve.

The officer guides me to the bottom stair in the entryway. "Sit before your legs give out." Cold air blows through the duct-taped screen door. He gives me a tissue when I sit down.

"Bri?"

I look up. Zinnia stands on the top stair clutching Mr. Hoppy. I leap up the stairs. She jumps into my arms before I reach the top. Her face is tear-streaked. I pull her close and sit on the top stair. Holding her tightly, I rock back and forth with her, cheek-to-cheek, and bury my nose in her hair. She smells like baby shampoo.

"Daddy was mad and yelling," she whimpers. "Mommy kept calling for you."

My throat tightens. "Did you stay in bed?"

She nods.

"Good girl."

"You weren't here," she says. Her tone is factual, not accusatory.

"I'm sorry." There has never been a time when I wasn't here for her. Or, Mom.

Zinnia studies my face. Her small finger reaches up and traces my right eye lid. "You have makeup on."

"Miss," the officer says, "is there someone you can call?"

"We'll be fine by ourselves."

"I'll have to call social services."

"I'm almost seventeen."

Zinnia tightens her grip around my neck.

"You'll do no such thing, Jerry," Val says. She's wearing an oversized parka. She stomps the snow from her white, calve-high snow boots and slams the door behind her. She struts past the officer as she pulls off her thick gloves.

"They're in my care now, so you just go about doing what you need to do."

"Val, this isn't your business."

"I'm making it my business."

"As you know, absent family in this situation, social services needs to be called. It's protocol."

"I'm their auntie."

"Come on, Val, you can't be auntie to everyone." His voice is soft, his expression sheepish. "Best if you stay out of this."

"You can't tell me I'm not their auntie. You wouldn't do that would you, Jerry?"

The officer sighs and shakes his head.

Val motions for us to come. "You'll come to my place until your Mom gets home."

At the bottom of the staircase, my eyes meet Brody's. "I didn't know who else to call when I saw the police taking your dad away," he says.

Twelve

VAL CONTACTS THE BEMIDJI HOSPITAL and learns that Mom's condition is serious but stable. As soon as Zinnia awakes, we begin the 20 minute drive to see Mom.

I hate hospitals: the smell of disinfectant; the glaring lights; the sad faces in the waiting areas, hallways and elevator; the doctors and nurses whispering; and people not seeing you or, if they do, looking away. Everyone is in their own hell that they didn't see coming-even if maybe they should have.

Hospital staff direct us to Mom's room on the third floor. She lays motionless beneath a thin, white blanket with a bandage wrapped around her head. Her purple, puffy eyes are closed. Tubes poke her limp, bruised arms. Beeps and flashing numbers come from a nearby machine. The other bed in the room is unoccupied.

Zinnia scales the front of my body and holds on for dear life. I stroke her hair and tell her that Mom's going to be alright, a truth I want to believe.

Before, Mom just covered the bruises with makeup and pretended everything was fine. We still knew who she was and that she'd be okay. Biting the inside of my mouth, I taste blood. I wish Dad was the one lying here. Or, better yet, dead. That way we'd never have to worry about him ever again.

A young nurse with an efficient gait enters carrying a Styrofoam pitcher. She places it on the brown, narrow table near the full plastic water glass with the bendy straw.

"I'm Stephanie, the nurse this shift." She points to her

name on the whiteboard. "The doctor is conducting rounds, but it shouldn't be too long before he stops by. Make yourself comfortable."

She checks the monitors and, using her badge, opens the computer on the stand near the bed and types something without explanation. As she's about to leave, she points out the call button on the remote, the same one we can use to turn on the TV.

Val strides to the white board and writes her name and cell number with the blue dry erase marker velcroed to the board. Then, she tosses a backpack onto the unused bed. "There's some cards, coloring books and snacks."

Zinnia lets me lower her onto the bed. She unzips the backpack and finds Old Maid cards and fruit roll-ups.

Val paces the room with crossed arms. Periodically, she positions herself in the doorway and looks down the hall, scowls, shakes her head and mutters something to herself. Then, she paces some more.

I turn on the TV and begin switching channels. When I land on the game show, Price is Right, Val plops into the reclining chair and says, "Keep it here."

Zinnia begs me to play Old Maid so I deal the cards.

"I'm going to win," Zinnia says smiling, holding the mass of cards in both hands. "You have the Old Maid."

"You don't know who will win. Just play."

We go back and forth.

I avoid looking over at Mom.

A pock-faced aide with a trimmed goatee brings us three oversized chocolate chip cookies. "These are still warm," he says before leaving. I grab a cookie and bite off a chunk. It's warm, but not the soft, gooey kind Mom makes. It doesn't even taste like real chocolate chips. I spit the mushy mouthful of cookie into a napkin.

I toss my cards down. "I don't want to play anymore. You win."

Zinnia pumps her small fists. Then, she spreads out all the cards and begins matching them while Val continues to blurt out answers and curse the contestants who don't guess correctly.

There's a People magazine in the backpack. I start flipping through the pages of famous, gorgeous people who are all smiles in their perfect lives. I come across a picture of Taylor Swift holding a white cat like a baby while strolling the streets of New York City.

The cat reminds me of the one I thought I killed when I was 14. Dad had thrown me outside when I tried to stop him from hitting Mom. The neighbor's cat, with its golden eyes and silky white fur, came over and would not leave me alone. It kept rubbing its narrow body against my leg and purring as the violence inside the house mounted. No matter how many times I pushed the cat away, it came back. I couldn't take it anymore and, without thinking, I kicked the cat. It laid still. I thought I killed it, but then it got up and slinked away into the shadows.

There's a soft knock on the door and a man, hunched over and looking nearly a hundred years old, introduces himself as Dr. Williams. He examines the cards on the bed through thick black rimmed eyeglasses. "You've done an excellent job here, young lady," he says to Zinnia. She buries her head behind my back.

Dr. Williams pulls over the chair near the computer and sits down. "She's sedated right now. There are no broken bones or cranial bleeding shown on the CT scan. But, she sustained brain trauma from the blows to her head. Without further diagnostic testing and observation, we won't know the long-term impact and prognosis. Given the bruising all over her body, we want to run tests to rule out any internal bleeding." He pauses, then says, "Considering everything, she's very lucky."

It's clear to me that Mom's luck is running out.

Thirteen

AFTER A WEEK OF TESTS and observation, Mom returns home today. Val pulls in front of our house without turning off the ignition. "Your mom is being discharged now. See if you can keep the house clean until we get back."

Zinnia and I get out and plod forward to the front door, our footsteps crunching the snow packed sidewalk. Dad's truck blocks Mom's car in the driveway. Snow covers both vehicles. My gloveless fingers tighten around Zinnia's small, mittened hand. Next door, Mrs. Winkelman's inflatable snowman bows in the wind. Our house is one of the few on the street without any Christmas decorations.

Guilt overwhelms me. I should've visited Mom more during her hospital stay. Sure, Zinnia needed care, but the truth is the visits were short and too infrequent because I couldn't bear to see Mom like that; it ripped my soul out.

Mom deserves a daughter who stayed by her side; held her hand and watched TV with her without even caring if she spoke; brushed her hair; lifted the bent straw to her swollen, dry, and cracked lips; and found the words, any words, to comfort her and say we'll be okay. Instead, Mom has me and it's my fault this happened to her. I snuck out and used Mom's phone to arrange it. How did I not think Dad would make her pay?

The house smells of Pine Sol and bleach. The glass from the broken mirror and Tiffany lamp are gone. Nails remain on the smoked-stained vacant walls.

"Presents!" Zinnia runs toward a midget tree in the corner near the front window. Silver tinsel dangles from its branches. An angel perches on top. Blue and white lights alternately blink. Boxes wrapped in shiny silver and gold paper rest against each other on a green and red plaid tree skirt.

The carpet's been vacuumed and smells like the powder you use to cover dog pee. Heavy, bone colored fabric hangs from a thick wooden rod. The panels, pulled aside, expose the tall snowbanks and gray sky.

Val said Brody asked, apparently more than once, to see me. That's not happening. Every time I think of him my stomach clenches and I feel like throwing up. It helps if I turn my thoughts to Dad rotting in jail for the rest of his life or someone beating him up (or worse).

It's not long before Zinnia squeals, "Mommy's here!"

Val opens the passenger door and helps Mom stand. She waits as Mom pauses, leans on the door frame and then takes baby steps toward the house. She's hunched over with her arm looped in Val's.

She looks old, like Grandma Rita. I still feel bad I never called her, but Mom wouldn't have wanted me to.

Zinnia hugs Mom's legs when she crosses the threshold. Mom's grimace is barely noticeable. She smiles and opens her arms when she sees me. I go to her and we have a three-way squeeze-way. She kisses my cheek.

It's hard to look at her bruised, sunken eyes. Val says Mom's bruises and head will heal. She's getting better every day, but it takes time. But, there are wounds you can't see. They're deep. Hidden behind smiles.

Zinnia takes Mom's hand and steers her toward the sparkly tree. "There's presents, Mommy. See?"

Frigid air drafts through the partially shut door. I press my back against the archway.

"Stairs will be harder for her, so go slow," Val mutters to me, as if she can read my mind. "I'm going to get her prescriptions filled and bring them by later. I'll get a plastic box with the days of the week and fill it with the morning and night meds. It'll make it easy. Just don't forget to give them to her on schedule. Got it?"

I nod.

"I almost forgot." Val opens her cavernous bag and starts digging. Then, she hands me an iPhone. It's new. The hard plastic case has the Hogwarts crest. She says, "I need to know you have a way to reach me in case you need to so I put you on my plan. It's not unlimited, so don't go crazy."

There's not a scratch or crack on the slim gold iPhone.

"I'm number one in your Favorites," she says, nudging my side.

I'm stunned.

She's gone before I can thank her. I turn on the phone and see the screensaver: Zinnia and I cuddled cheek-to-cheek on Val's soft, moss colored couch. Zinnia's wide smile proudly shows the gap in front where she lost her first tooth this week. My hard eyes resemble my dad's.

Fourteen

I HELP MOM SHOWER on her third day home. She wraps her arm around me for support and stiffly steps over the tub's side. I join her, closing the curtain. Mom faces the shower head while I stand behind her wearing a one-piece swimsuit.

Mom grimaces as she lifts her arms so I gently lather her hair with Zinnia's baby shampoo. Then, she tips her head slightly backwards to rinse. As Mom cleans her body, the bar slips out of her hands. I bend down to pick it up, afraid I might inadvertently touch one of her many deep purple bruises.

Water cascades over us for a long time. Finally, I reach around Mom and turn off the faucet, open the shower curtain, and then step outside and wait. When Mom steps onto the beige bathmat, I drape the soft flowered beach towel over her bony shoulders. She gazes forward at nothing in particular.

Wrapped in the beach towel, Mom shuffles to her bedroom, and sits on the edge of the bed. I hold up the knee-length nightgown Val brought her. Mom releases the towel and raises her arms slightly. I slip her arms through the sleeves of the oversized nightgown, then maneuver it over her head. The violet fabric is a soft, worn cotton with small white flowers. It's something an old person would wear. Mom doesn't ask for underwear and I don't offer or suggest any.

The shower exhausts Mom. She stiffly lowers herself backward onto the bed as I carefully lift her legs. During the process, she squeezes her eyes shut and winces. After placing an extra pillow beneath her legs, I wait to see what she needs next. I've learned it takes time for her to get past the pain and find the words to express what she wants.

Mom says, "Will you please put lotion on my legs? They're so dry."

As I gently rub it on Mom's thin calves, I look at the picture on the nightstand of Mom and Dad from their senior prom. Dad, with short black hair and well-trimmed sideburns, has his arm around Mom's waist. She's dressed in a sleeveless honey colored chiffon dress. Golden ringlets dangle on her rosy cheeks and pink gloss highlights her full lips. It's the only picture I've seen where he's smiling.

Mom's eyes open when I stop rubbing her legs. She whispers, "Please don't hate him." Then, without waiting for a promise I can't make, her eyes close.

I lower onto the floor. My hand bumps a photo album sticking out from under the bed. It's been ages since I went through the albums Mom made when she and Grandma Rita were into scrapbooking. This was before their last big fight over Dad and we could no longer see or talk to her.

I flip quickly through the pages. Most bore me, but one catches my attention. It's from the day I was born. Mom is holding me, swaddled in a pink blanket and knit hat, while Dad sits on the edge of the hospital bed looking down at me. My finger curls around his pinkie. "He was so proud to be your daddy," Mom said the first time we looked at this picture.

I rip Dad out of the picture and tear him to bits.

Fifteen

I RETURN TO SCHOOL after nearly two weeks. I dodge people in the halls, head down and backpack strapped over both shoulders. It feels like countless eyes follow me. I'm no longer the new girl. I'm *that* girl. Be careful, I'm sure they are thinking, she's the one with the crazy, homicidal prone dad. And, you know the expression: the fruit usually doesn't fall far from the tree. Wacko. Steer clear.

Ms. O'Brien, my AP English teacher, doesn't believe in assigned seating. She encourages students to "mix it up" every day because she thinks rigidity stifles creativity. I choose a desk with a view out the window.

There's a writing prompt on the whiteboard. I take out my composition notebook and begin the assignment. The desk wobbles. I don't bother taking a piece of paper, folding it, and tucking it under the uneven leg.

I keep my head down as voices fill the room. Hair flops into my face as I write. Crap fills the pages. I don't care. No one ever sees it and, even if they did, I wouldn't care.

I flinch when someone touches my arm. Maddy's flawless complexion and bright smile greet me. "I wondered when you'd come back. We've been worried about you."

We?

She claims the desk next to mine. Normally she sits in front, a prime teacher's pet location. "You okay? I would have reached out, but you don't have a phone."

I don't tell her about the phone Val gave me. I tuck my hair behind my ear. No one should have such clear skin. Have I ever seen her with a pimple?

"It must be hard," she says, "Anything I can do?"

"Nope." I hope she'll get the hint as I resume writing rubbish in the notebook.

"How about hanging out this weekend?"

I put my pen down and look at her. "Seriously, Maddy, you don't have to be nice to me. Really. I'm fine." I think I actually sound convincing.

Maddy looks like she's going to cry. She whispers, "Evan dumped me. I thought we could talk, maybe lean on each other?"

I sigh deeply. "I'm pretty busy."

"Saturday?"

"I promised to make cookies with Zinnia." It is the best excuse I can come up with. No one wants to hang out with a kid sister.

Maddy's eyes light up. "Yum. Cookies." Her imitation of the Cookie Monster on Sesame Street attracts Ms. O'Brien's glare. Maddy's unfazed. She smiles sweetly, takes her notebook out and begins writing.

I mentally make a list of all the reasons why Maddy shouldn't come to our house. Mom's face is still bruised and she walks like Frankenstein. Also, our place is a slum compared to Maddy's. None of the furniture matches and the carpet smells like wet dog even though we don't have one.

Despite all these reasons, I pass Maddy a note as the bell rings and invite her over on Saturday at one o'clock to make cookies. I give her my phone number. Without waiting to see her reaction, I bolt out of the classroom.

I'm not even to my locker before Maddy texts me a string of happy emojis.

sixteen

THICK SNOW FALLS STEADILY on Saturday until there's no visible distinction between the boulevard and street. It's a seamless blanket. I paint Zinnia's nails as Christmas music plays from my phone.

"Why isn't she here yet?"

I check to see if Maddy's sent a text. There's none.

"She'll be here when she's here." I push aside the brown paper bag protecting the kitchen table from pink polish drips. "Do you like them?"

Zinnia nods and blows on her nails.

The ingredients for chocolate chip cookies with green and red sprinkles are set out on the Formica counter. A cinnamon-orange candle flickers in a glass jar next to the sink.

A plow rumbles past the house. Only a white wall of blowing snow is visible from the kitchen window. I rise and put the butter back into the fridge.

The doorbell rings. Zinnia squeals and runs into the hallway. She flings both the wood and storm doors open.

Maddy, rosy cheeked, comes in wearing a short waisted purple ski coat and coordinated Beanie stocking hat.

Zinnia threads her hand in mine. "We didn't think you were coming, did we, Bri?"

"Sorry," Maddy says. Snowflakes tip her long, curling lashes. "Did you start without us?"

"Us?"

"When I told Brody that I was coming over to make cookies, he insisted on picking me up and coming too."

Brody clomps up the steps looking like a Yeti, sporting a parka and full, untrimmed beard.

"He said he'd love to help with the cookies. Isn't that sweet?"

I manage a smile.

Zinnia is captivated with Maddy's nails, which we learn are French tipped acrylic nails. Her mom takes her to the nail salon in Bemidji. Apparently, it's a step up from the local one, and certainly better than nails polished on a paper bag.

Maddy takes charge, overseeing the measuring and mixing of the ingredients according to the recipe on the back of the Toll House chocolate chip bag. Zinnia clings to Maddy, her new best friend. Brody rambles on about the boys' basketball team destined to win State. When I pass him an egg, it drops and splats on the table. Maddy snatches a handful of paper napkins and scoops up the slimy mess and deposits it in the garbage under the sink. I hand him another egg and he cracks it into the bowl. He beats the butter, sugars, eggs and vanilla in the silver bowl while Maddy mixes the dry ingredients in a chipped porcelain bowl.

I watch, do as I'm told, and say as little as possible.

Mom drags something across the floor upstairs. Maddy and Brody stop bantering and look toward the ceiling.

"Go check on Mom," I say to Zinnia. She reluctantly goes upstairs after we promise not to eat any cookies without her.

Maddy and Brody spoon dough onto the cookie sheet while I alternate red and green sprinkles.

"You should come to the games sometime," Brody says. "Fan support really helps."

"Maybe. We could be gone tomorrow." I mutter as I put

the filled cookie sheet into the oven, "And, that would be fine with me. I hate this town."

"There are worse places," Brody says.

I set the timer on my phone. "I doubt it."

Maddy throws the teaspoon into the silver mixing bowl and glares at me. "Do you take that sulky I'm-better-than-you shit whenever you go?"

Brody laughs awkwardly.

"I have tried to be your friend." Maddy's voice is shaky. "And, I'm trying now. But, you don't seem to care."

"If you hadn't noticed, I got some things going on."

"Even before that. You acted like you're better than us. Maybe we're not cool like your friends in Minneapolis. But, we're not all Northwoods losers."

Brody says, "Dial it down, Maddy. You'll miss out on that friend-of-the-year award."

My cheeks burn. "What difference does it make to you whether I like you or anyone else in this God forsaken town?"

Maddy's blue eyes water. "Everyone's got shit in their lives."

"Your life looks pretty perfect to me."

"We're not all bad."

"I never said you were."

"We just want to help." Maddy plays with the locket around her neck, refusing to look at me.

"I'm doing fine without your help."

Maddy stares out the window with a hard look on her puckered face. "Whatever."

The radiator clanks. Sticky, thick silence hangs between us. I open the oven to check the cookies. The centers are still raw. I check to see how much time is left, then open Instagram and spin through strangers' posts.

Brody breaks the silence. "Did you hear that Coach Anhorn got married?" Both Maddy and I look at him. "Yeah, to a dude."

Maddy's eyes widen. "How do you know these things?"

Brody motions like he's zipping his lips.

Maddy forgets she's mad at me and proceeds on the school gossip train. Most of the people I don't know, or really care about, but I'm relieved for the shift in conversation. At some point Maddy mentions that Dirk was asking her about me.

Brody scowls. "He's trouble."

"Oh, he's not that bad, just a little full of himself," Maddy says.

"All guys start off pretending to be decent," I say, "then wind up jerks."

Brody says, "Hey, how come all guys get a bad rap?"

The timer chimes. I get up to retrieve the cookies from the oven. When I return to the table, I ask Brody, "What's up with the beard?"

"No-Shave November, baby," he announces proudly.

Maddy says, "It's supposed to raise awareness and money for cancer. But, it's now an excuse to go wild and hairy."

"But, it's December."

"Ah, yes, but," Brody pauses and holds up his finger like he has an important point to make. "There's a very practical side that you wouldn't appreciate. Protection against the cold."

Maddy says, "Somehow we survive."

"You're jealous," Brody teases.

All of a sudden Maddy and Brody stop talking and their smiles disappear.

Mom's standing in the doorway dressed in a turtleneck sweater, which covers the remaining bruises on her neck.

She's dug out a black leather skirt with matching leggings, and low heels. It looks more like she's going to a party rather than coming downstairs for cookies.

"Hey, kids." Mom's lopsided smile is painted with shimmering gloss. Her chipped tooth is visible. "It sounds like you're having fun." Faint blue shadow glitters on Mom's lids. The thick foundation doesn't fully cover her bruises.

Zinnia skips in. "See Mommy, there's a boy."

Mom wraps her spindly arm around me. "It's nice of you to come over and see Bridget. She's been such an old mother hen. She could use some fun."

I pull away. "Shouldn't you be resting or something?"

Mom stiffly lowers onto a chair. "I wanted to meet your friends."

Maddy says, "We were just talking about school stuff."

"Boys?"

"Mom!"

"What? That's what I talked about when I was your age."

"They don't care." My eyes beg her to stop.

Brody and Maddy exchange glances as Mom bites into a warm, gooey cookie. An awkward silence lingers. Then, Maddy rises. "We really should go," she says. "I told my mom we wouldn't stay long with it snowing like it is."

"Yeah, it's not letting up," Brody chimes in.

Mom looks disappointed. "Maybe you can come again? We could order pizza next time?"

"That'd be great," Maddy says with feigned enthusiasm.

When I get up, Maddy says, "No, don't. You stay with your mom. We know the way out." She comes over, gives me a hug and, says in a whispered voice close to my ear, "Sorry I was a jerk. I just got my period."

"Me too," I say. "I mean, about being a jerk."

seventeen

THE SNOW CRUNCHES beneath my feet as I walk to the Bait and Thrift on the afternoon of New Year's Eve. I push the door open; the blended aroma of minnows and Sandalwood incense greets me.

Val sits on a stool at the cash register playing Solitaire in a Hawaiian themed top that exposes her fully tattooed arms. "Look who the cat dragged in," she says, flipping and moving cards.

"I needed to get out."

"I'm honored."

"There's nowhere else to go."

"*Was* honored."

"Sorry."

Her laugh is deep and throaty. "No offense taken. Have a seat."

The three-legged metal stool scrapes across the discolored, dirty linoleum floor when I pull it over. My chest is barely level with the counter. There's drumming music playing.

Val moves a group of cards. "Seen Brody lately?" Her bifocals perch on her wide nose.

"We're on winter break, remember?"

"People see each other on breaks. You have a phone too."

I pick up a package of plastic strawberry scented worms from the display and thoroughly examine it. My fingers squeeze their soft bodies. "Say, do you think you could use help here?"

Val's thickly lined eyes squint. "I dunno. This is pretty intellectually challenging work. How are your grades?"

"B's, but I'll get them back to A's."

"That might be too good for here. The other staff might get intimidated."

"Who else works here?"

"Just me. And, I can be a pain in the ass."

I can't help but laugh. "Really? I hadn't noticed."

The bell jingles. A hunched old man in a one-piece insulated coverall enters wearing a wool hat with ear flaps. Cold air follows.

Val puts the cards away. "Hey, Earl, what's cookin'?"

He stomps snow from thick rubbered brown boots and removes his snowmobile gloves. "Ed and me were fishing and ran out of propane. Just when they were biting."

"Grab what you need," Val says.

"Only the propane. Oh, and a gaff hook. I dropped mine in the hole, wouldn't you know."

"They're on the shelf over there, by the tip-ups and line."

Earl pays cash for the items and promises to come by later with filets if their luck turns. The wind's shifting, he explains, and that's never good.

After Earl leaves, Val asks, "How's your mom?"

"She got out of bed for Christmas." I pick at an ingrown fingernail. "But, she still cries a lot."

Val places her hand on mine. "My first husband, Alfred, used me as a punching bag. Still, I loved that bastard and kept letting him come back. I didn't care what it took to keep him. Even if it cost me my kids. And, it did."

A lump in my throat prevents me from speaking.

"Life's hard and it sure as hell doesn't get easier, let me tell you. But, there are worse things than being alone." She points her long shiny red nail at me. "Like knowing that you could have been a good mom and will never get that chance again."

Val grabs an unopened pack of Natural American Spirit cigarettes on the shelf behind her and a glass ashtray with the Big Dipper Casino's insignia. The plastic crinkles. Drawing a cigarette to her lips, she flicks the lighter. Smoke lofts toward the discolored ceiling tiles.

An Amber Alert blares from our phones. Val shifts her bifocals and squints at her phone. "A 12-year-old girl abducted. Not far from the casino." Releasing a deep sigh, she says, "They're probably long gone by now and she won't be coming home." She smashes the unfinished cigarette in the clean ashtray.

My phone pings. "Maddy's almost here to pick me up."

"Aren't you the social butterfly," Val says. "You can start here next Saturday at 10 a.m. Don't be late. That pisses me off."

"Thanks. You don't even have to pay me much."

"I wasn't planning on it."

"I thought we might draw today," Maddy says, presenting an unopened box of dry erase markers. The far wall in the lower level is bare. "Mom put a new coat of dry erase paint on the wall. Apparently, I'm to use better judgement in what I put on it."

Opening the box, I reach for the red marker, which smells faintly fruity, and begin drawing as music plays from the Bose speaker. Skipper sprawls on his back near us.

Maddy sits cross-legged. "Did you ever find the chocolates I dropped off on Christmas?"

"Yeah, sorry. Zinnia went crazy over them. Didn't I text you?" I don't tell her that I didn't even think about getting her a gift.

Maddy flicks a dismissive wave. "No worries. I'm glad you found them. It wasn't much, but I wanted to give you something." Thankfully, she doesn't ask what I got for Christmas or share what most likely was a mound of presents she received.

We draw mostly without talking. Maddy's marker choices and sketching movements are quick and decisive while I'm slow, tentative and detailed. She frequently shuffles the music, choosing artists I've heard but can't name.

With a flare, she proclaims, "Ta-da", as she adds a smiley face on the sun that has straight lines shooting from its round center.

"Nice."

"Obviously, I can't compete with you," Maddy says. "Is that a flower garden? And, a castle?"

"I guess."

"Where did you learn to draw like that?"

"My grandma studied and taught art. We used to hang out and do art projects." My finger erases a leaf I've messed up. "I miss her."

Maddy scratches Skipper's belly. "My grandma worked at the church rectory and ran bingo on Sunday evenings. She snuck me free cards when I was young, but I never won."

Skipper loudly passes gas and we burst out laughing. Maddy pushes him away and reclines against the sectional's ottoman.

"You talk to Brody lately?"

"Why would I?"

"I thought maybe you guys liked each other?"

"What makes you think that?"

"Well, after, you know, the thing with your dad, he kept asking about you, wondering if you were okay. He really wanted to come and make cookies at your place. I thought maybe there was something going on between you guys."

Maddy's wide eyes search my face.

"Nope," I say, focusing on the wall.

A strand of hair from Maddy's French braid falls soft on her face. She twirls it around her finger. "So, you don't like him?"

"Why we still talking about this?"

"Well, I might be interested in him if you're not."

I shove the marker into the box. "He's all yours."

Eighteen

DAD'S CUDDLING MOM on the couch when Zinnia and I return home from the first day of school after Christmas break. Zinnia runs over and jumps into his lap.

"God, you got big." He acts like he can barely hold her as he cradles her back and forth. Zinnia runs her hands back and forth over his hair, now buzzed short.

I stand in the doorway with my canvas backpack heavy over both shoulders. Cold air seeps under the door and into the entryway.

Mom says, "Isn't it great that Daddy's home?"

I don't dare speak the words I'm thinking.

Dad comes over, Zinnia still clinging to him, and wraps his arm around my shoulder. "Hey kiddo." He pulls me in while my arms hang limp at my sides.

"I'm starving," Dad says. "What's there to eat?"

Mom immediately jumps up. She's wearing jeans that once fit but now are baggy on her pencil thin legs. When she asks me if I will help make dinner, I drop my backpack, kick it to the corner and follow her into the kitchen.

Brown paper bags full of groceries are on the kitchen table. I begin putting them away. Mom opens the lower cabinet where she stores cooking pans of various sizes. As she searches for the right one, they bang against each other.

Mom starts humming as she gets hamburger from the refrigerator. Her hair, normally curly and lately unwashed, is straightened. She's wearing makeup and silver hoop earrings.

"So, he's out of jail?" I pull out a chair and look down at the cloth placemat that has a hardened bit of pizza cheese on its edge. I pick at it with my fingernail. "I mean, for good?"

"Honey, I hope so, but there's people who want to lock him up for a long time." She begins filling the stock pot with water. "The hotshot prosecutor wants to make a name for herself. They don't care what I want."

Four plates are stacked in the center of the table. I reach over and put a plate on each mat. "Is he going to stay here?"

Mom looks surprised. "Of course. Where else?"

I don't answer and finish setting the table. From the other room, I can hear Dad cursing at the TV.

I recall when I used to watch hockey games on TV with him when I was Zinnia's age. I could rarely follow the puck on the small screen, only the bulky players speeding down the ice and slamming each other into the boards. But I loved how he'd let me sit in his lap. He'd try and explain the rules and I'd pretend to understand them. I hated it when the game ended.

Mom browns the hamburger and onions. She adds two jars of Ragu sauce. Steam rises from the boiling water and condenses on the window above the sink.

The kitchen smells like a real meal, something we haven't had for a while. Mom focuses on dumping the noodles into the boiling water and stirring them so they don't stick together-one of Dad's pet peeves. She jumps when the doorbell rings.

"I'll get it," I say. Passing the living room on the way to the front door, I see Zinnia snuggled next to Dad. The sun is setting so the room is cloaked in shifting shadows.

Jags struts past me when I open the door. "My man, how the hell are you?"

Dad rises and fist bumps him. "Thanks for bailing me out, bro."

"Hell, yeah. Sorry it took so long." Jags takes off the "A.J.'s Taxidermy" hat and scratches thinning hair that falls limply on his narrow face that's shadowed by a thin, graying beard. "Wasn't sure how to make it work. But it's done and here you are."

Dad casts a glance toward the kitchen. "Bring anything?"

"Later, man. But, I got this." Jags takes out a bottle of Jim Beam out of his jacket and Dad hollers for Mom to bring glasses.

I duck back into the kitchen as Mom bursts out with two low glasses.

Hot steam rises from the stock pot. I stare at the boiling water, frequently testing the noodles. When they're done, I lift the large pot off the burner and tilt it so the steamy water and noodles dump into the strainer lodged in the sink. It slips and scalding water splashes onto my hands.

I drop the pot and cry out.

No one hears me. Or, if they do, they don't come. Or, care.

Tears stream down my face. My skin burns. I want to scream, but, I know that won't do any good. I turn on the cold water, place my scalded hands under its stream, close my eyes, and wait for the pain to go away.

Nineteen

A THIN WALL separates our bedroom from my parents. Clamping the pillow around my ears, I cocoon under the heavy pile of blankets with Zinnia glued to my side. No matter what song I try to play in my head I can't block out the headboard banging against the wall or the commingled moans.

It was easier listening to Mom's endless sobbing.

I finally get out of bed, careful not to wake Zinnia. Mr. Hoppy's ear is pressed against her rosy cheek. She tried staying up until Dad came back from his "quick" trip somewhere with Jags. Thankfully, she fell asleep before he came home and I don't have to try to explain the reunion I'm experiencing through the wall.

I tiptoe down the stairs, careful to dodge the creaky spots. I retrieve the afghan from the floor and tuck it under my legs like a mermaid as I settle into the sunken center of the couch.

Flipping through the channels, I land on the final Harry Potter movie. I know every word from reading the Harry Potter books and seeing all the movies more times than I can count.

Harry's battle with Voldemort rages. I pretend not to notice Dad standing in the archway wearing only his boxers. He retreats into the kitchen, but soon returns with two cans of Budweiser beer and a bag of Cheetos. Instead of going upstairs or sitting in the La-Z-Boy recliner, he lumbers to the couch.

"Move over," he says.

The afghan slides to the floor when I sit up and squeeze next to the couch's threadbare arm. He sits on the opposite end and sets the Cheetos between us. "Have some. You know you want them."

I ignore him and the Cheetos. I keep waiting for Dad to demand the remote as he hates Harry Potter. But, he watches the movie without comment and eats the Cheetos.

After draining his beer, he cracks the other and thrusts it into my hand. "You can have this one." He rises, returning to the kitchen.

I was in the third grade when Dad gave me my first beer. Graffiti defaced the brick exterior of the bar we drove to. There were no windows, only a dented steel door. Dad told me to sit and keep my mouth shut while he talked to his friends. The smoke burned my eyes and throat. We were there a long time. When I started coughing and couldn't quit, he told the bartender to get him a glass. Then he poured beer into the glass and told me to drink it. I choked on the bitter taste, but my coughing subsided. When the glass emptied, he poured more into it. I don't remember leaving the bar, only waking to vomit in my bed.

That was my last beer until the party at Evan's.

Dad returns from the kitchen with another beer and plops onto the couch. "I've been thinking that you need to learn to drive."

"The class costs money."

"I never took a damn class. I'll take you out. There's plenty of roads going nowhere here that you can practice on."

"I got other things to do."

"That right? Are you Miss Popular now? Or, have a boyfriend?"

His eyes demand an answer.

I shake my head "no" and take a small sip of beer even though I told myself I wouldn't.

Grandma Rita once told me I talked with my eyes. She made it sound like a superpower. Like Harry Potter resisting Voldemort's efforts to invade his head, I use all my powers to not let Dad see what I'm thinking.

A Cheeto hits my cheek.

"I sure as hell hope you don't have a boyfriend," Dad says. There's no playful or teasing smile. The message is unmistakable.

Twenty

I ESCAPE THE HOUSE on Saturday morning before anyone is up. It's my first day officially working at the Bait and Thrift. The sun shines for the first time in an eternity and, even though it's mid-January and the air is frosty, it feels warm on my face.

Arriving before Val, I sit on the top step. Black birds cluster in the flat bottomed bird feeder hanging from a chain on the lower branch of the crab apple tree in front. Squirrels scramble below, scavenging discarded seeds in the snow.

Val finally arrives.

"Lordy, you look like you lost your best friend."

"Dad's home."

A deep crease forms between her thick lined eyes. "Just blew through the restraining order?"

This is the first I've heard of a restraining order.

Val lumbers up the three wooden stairs, her mammoth purse hanging from the crux of her arm. She's wearing a brown furry hat with flaps covering her ears. She pauses to catch her breath before unlocking the door. Inside, she flicks on the lights and motions me to follow her through the dangling glass beads to the back room.

Val strips her parka and wool scarf off. "I'll make some calls. I know the prosecutor, Peg. She's tough. But, there's only so much she can do if your mom lets him waltz through the damn door."

I sit on a metal folding chair beside the round card table

piled with untagged clothes and take off my coat. Val fills the coffeemaker with tap water. She retrieves the Folgers can and a paper filter from the shelf. When she tips the can to fill the basket, some grounds fall onto the floor. As she sweeps, her hips move to the broom's motions.

"I've been thinking," I begin, but then stop, regretting even entertaining the thought I was prepared to present.

Val props her arms on the broom as she looks at me, perhaps miffed I interrupted her broom dance. "You expect me to read your mind?"

"It's not that big of a deal."

She waits for me to speak, clearly impatient.

"I was just remembering that you said you worked at Aveda in Minneapolis and cut hair before moving back here. Maybe, you could cut my hair?"

"You want your ends trimmed?"

I run my fingers through the ends of my straight mousy hair. It's parted in the middle and falls past my shoulders. "Short."

She looks amused. "That so?" Maybe she's questioning my sanity. I know I am. I've never had short hair. No one I know has short hair.

"If you want short hair, you get short hair."

I consider changing my mind, but there's no going back. As Grandma Rita used to say, "It's too late to stop the train once it's out of the station."

Val soon returns with her "Authentic Japanese Hitachi" cutting shears and wraps a flowered bed sheet around my shoulders. She examines my head from different directions before taking the shears out of their special case. She's a fiend with the shears, snipping fast and furious like she's racing the clock. Dark hair soon covers the floor.

I close my eyes, afraid to face what I fear is a big mistake.

Part of me wishes there was a mirror to see how it looks, while the other part knows I'd only panic more. I can't help wondering if my ears will look like Dumbo's now that they're exposed.

The cutting slows. Val checks the evenness of the hair on the top and sides. "Not many can pull it off, but you can." She surveys her handiwork. "It actually suits you. Your eyes pop."

Val insists on applying makeup. She glides silky liquid black liner on my eyelids, then soft shadow, and finally powdery blush on my cheeks.

"Gorgeous. Go check out the finished package."

I go to the full length mirror on the wall near the makeshift dressing room with trepidation. When I see myself, I can't help but smile.

"Brody will flip when he sees you," Val says.

"Hardly."

"He's a good egg."

"I don't care for eggs."

"I've had my share of bad eggs, and, while the bad ones can spoil your taste for them, it's only for a while. Then, you go craving them again."

Sometimes it's hard to understand Val's pearls of wisdom.

"I prefer Loops."

Val's laugh is deep until she starts coughing. She withdraws a tissue from her bra and spits a thick wad of something into the tissue.

"You okay?"

"At seventy-one, I'm happy being upright." She tosses the tissue in the plastic waste bin and settles on the stool. "Your dad behaving himself?"

"Who knows? A guy named Jags bailed him out and stopped over last night. They went somewhere after dinner. But he's home so Mom's happy."

"Jags from AJ's Taxidermy?"

"He wears a hat from there."

"Narrow face and dark beady eyes? Looks a little like a graying weasel?"

I nod.

Val scoffs. "Al Jaeger. He hangs around the reservation doing nothing good that I can see. How does your dad know him?"

I shrug, then glance around the room. The tables are piled high with clothes and lacking any organization. "What do you want me to do today? Fold clothes?"

"Brody's coming to help move these tables. My back won't hold up to it. He should be here any minute."

I quickly wipe off the shadow on my lids.

Val's eyes narrow. "Something up with you two?"

"No, my friend, Maddy, likes him."

"That so? Well, I hope she doesn't break his heart. He's a softy. Always has been. He sucked his thumb into middle school, but no one knew. Only did it when he was tired and thought no one was looking." She shakes her long, red-painted nail at me. "Now, don't go telling him I said that."

I ask the question I've been wondering. "Why are you and Brody so close if you've never been family?"

Val sighs. "Brody's mom took off when Brody was seven. He needed a mom, and I needed to mother after my kids weren't mine anymore."

As Val gets out her phone to text Brody, he steps through the dangling beads.

He stops in his tracks. "Whoa. Your hair is short."

"Your powers of perception are truly remarkable," Val says. "Where you been? I almost got worried."

"Dad started talking and I couldn't shut him up." Brody

takes his letter jacket off and tosses it on the metal folding chair next to me.

Val glances at her watch. "I have errands to do. While I'm gone, move the tables and work on the list by the coffee pot." She tosses us each a serving sized bag of Ruffles sour cream potato chips. "Here's pre-payment." She then leaves us alone, which terrifies me. I haven't been alone with him since sneaking out and all that went down.

Brody sits down on the folding chair. Given his size, it looks like he's sitting on those miniature chairs from grade school. "You going to the game tonight?"

I shake my head. "Dad's back."

His eyes widen. "Damn."

"His friend bailed him out so he's home until his trial."

"That blows. I'm sorry. How's it going?"

"So far he's still on his best behavior. We'll see how long that lasts."

Brody opens the bag of chips. "We're probably going to lose tonight anyway. A lot of our players are out with injuries."

"Maddy says you're getting a lot of playing time and leading in scoring. I hear there's been some recruiters at the games from Bemidji State and North Dakota. That's awesome."

"Doesn't much matter. Dad says the military needs guys like me and I owe it to my country. Plus, he thinks it'll look bad if the Army recruiter's son doesn't enlist."

"What do you want to do?"

Brody shrugs. His frayed jeans hug his muscular thighs. He looks intently at the pile of unsorted clothes between us.

"If you could do anything, what would it be?"

"Well," he says hesitantly, "If you could make a living fishing, I'd do that."

I can't help but laugh. "Ice fishing as a career?"

"Naw, ice fishing is for fun. Bass fishing during the warm weather, here in the summer, and then down south in the winter."

"I didn't know that was a thing." I recall our time in the icehouse and what could have happened between us. I say in a fake perky voice, "Have you taken Maddy ice fishing?"

"Yeah, a couple of times," he says matter-of-factly. "She doesn't really like to fish. Mostly, she talks."

I decide to toss out a line to snag some self-serving information. "She says you're getting serious."

"Really? She said that?"

"Well, not in so many words." Time to backtrack. I tell him what I do know: "She really likes you."

Brody stares at his fingers as he cracks them one by one. "Don't get me wrong. She's really hot. It's just that she talks a lot about herself and other people. You know?"

I did.

"Do you think I should talk to her? I don't want to lead her on."

Val strides through the beads. "What you two talking about?"

"Nothing," Brody says, looking down.

"He was telling me about fishing."

"Ah, yes, he can cook fish. Of course, I inspired him."

"Hardly. You burned everything you touched."

"That doesn't mean I didn't inspire you. Inspiration comes from different sources. If I hadn't cooked, you might not have taken any initiative. So, you're welcome."

I listen to Brody and Val banter back and forth. It's easy and light, not like Dad's barbed wire teasing.

I join in.

Brody jokes that I should join the Army with my new buzz cut. I fling my chip bag at him. It misses his head by a long shot. He recovers it, takes aim and flings it back at me.

"You don't know who you're messing with."

"You don't either," I say, smiling and running my hand through my hair.

It's not the only thing that feels lighter.

Twenty-One

THE NEXT MORNING Mom and I are peeling apples at the kitchen table when Dad strides into the kitchen just after noon. A cigarette hangs from his mouth and smoke trails him. A sneer crosses his dark stubbled jaw as he looks at me.

"You look like a God damned lesbian," he says. "Who said you could cut your hair?"

I grab a bright red apple without looking at him or answering.

Mom puts a mug of steaming coffee in front of him. "It'll grow back."

Dad takes a sip and scowls. "This shit been in the pot since last week?"

"No, I made it this morning."

Slowly, with a paring knife, I circle the blade around the outside of the apple.

"For Christ's sake, all I want is one decent cup of coffee. Is that too much to ask?"

Discarded peels fall onto a paper napkin. I halve the apple. Inside, the core is rotten. I set it aside and grab another. It appears perfect on the surface.

"I'll make another pot. It'll only take a minute."

"You'd think you were the Queen of England, sitting around eating bon bons, while I try to figure out how the hell we're supposed to eat and keep the lights on. One decent cup of coffee. That's all I wanted from you. You'd think you could do something right."

I dig the small blade in and gut the seeds. The white flesh, while slightly bruised in one section, is better than the last one. Apple peels and discarded innards mount and the juices soak through the napkin.

Poking at apple bits with the paring knife, I remember the time I asked Dad to show me how to whittle. Some boys in my fourth grade class were bragging about how their dads taught them. Dad agreed and said I was actually not bad with a knife.

Peeling back a strip of the apple's tough skin, I cut off the bad bit, and pop a chunk into my mouth. It's tart but juicy.

Dad's fist slams the table. "God dammit." He swipes the peelings to the floor. "Listen to me when I talk to you."

Our eyes meet. My knuckles whiten around the knife's silver handle. My breath rises, then lodges in my throat. I don't say anything for what seems forever. Then, I push back the chair, stand, and step over the peelings scattered on the dull, yellowed linoleum.

I go to Mom, who is clutching the counter like it's holding her up, and hand her the knife. "I'm done."

Dad rises and blocks the door as I head toward it.

"Where do you think you're going?" His stale, smoky breath washes over me. Every muscle in my body tightens. My jaw locks shut. He says, menacingly, "I. Asked. You. A. Question."

Rooted, with arms crossed over my chest, I remain silent, without turning away or averting his angry, bloodshot eyes.

His hand rises. "You think you're going to disrespect me in my own house?"

"Go ahead. Let's see what happens," I say. "You might have a hard time explaining to the police, lawyer, judge-whoever-that you don't deserve to be locked up if you lay one finger on me or Mom right now, especially with that restraining order no one here gives a shit about."

"Who do you think you are?" His icy tone dares me to defy him.

"It's the truth isn't it? Should I wear your bruises to school and see what they do?"

He sneers. "You think you're so smart."

It's like the showdown between Harry and Voldemort.

"I'm smarter than you think," I say, squeezing past him and out the kitchen. Without a backward glance, I grab my coat and slam the front door shut behind me.

Twenty-Two

THE BRANCHES OF THE LARGE OAK TREES lining the boulevard bow under the weight of last night's heavy snow. There's the sound of scraping shovels and growly snowblowers. The sidewalk is knee deep. I take to the unplowed street to walk in the tire tracks.

I haven't walked far when a horn startles me. For a minute my heart races. Has Dad followed me?

A rusted blue Chevy Impala slows beside me. The partially cleared window rolls down. It is Dirk. "Hey," he says. "What's up?"

"Walking," I say, turning to look over my shoulder. Dirk's car is the only one on the street.

"I can see you're walking."

"Then why ask?"

"Kinda testy, aren't you?"

"You really don't want to talk to me right now."

"I can give you a ride to wherever you're going. It's a helluva lot warmer in here."

I turn to look at him. He's not bad looking even with the freckles plastering his pale skin.

It's cold so I get in.

Dirk swipes the Copenhagen tobacco tin and Burger King wrappers to the floor so I can sit on the seat patched with duct tape. I kick aside the clutter and lean against the door.

"Where ya heading?" He flashes an over-confident grin. His teeth strike me as unusually white.

"Nowhere. I needed fresh air."

"Well, fresh it is. The air temperature's going to start dropping this afternoon with the Alberta clipper that's coming through. Best to get that walk in now or you'll freeze your sweet ass."

"Thanks for the meteorological update."

"Damn. I sounded like my dad."

"Well, if I start sounding like my dad, shoot me," I say.

The scene in the kitchen replays in my mind. Next time Dad might not exercise restraint. His fuse is dangerously near the surface. He erupts often despite near constant efforts on everyone's part to pacify him and deflect any potential triggers. Maybe Dad will be on his best behavior until his hearing? If I was a betting person, I wouldn't take those odds.

"Hello? You and Maddy going to the basketball game tonight or not?"

"Oh, sorry. No, I can't. I've got lots to do."

Dirk looks unconvinced, but drops the subject and turns on the radio. Ariana Grande is singing. I change the station. Country music crap is playing, but it's better. He smiles and reaches for my hand, which is lying in my lap. I'm too stunned to pull it back. No boy has ever held my hand.

Leaving town, we pass a billboard with a young Native girl gagged and staring at us with the words, "What if she was your daughter? See Evil? Hear Evil? Speak! Her Life could depend on it."

The roads look the same: flat, snow covered and desolate.

"Where are we going?"

His thumb circles the side of my hand. It feels like sandpaper, but light as a feather. "Want to go to my house? We could watch TV and hang out."

There are so many reasons why this isn't a good idea.

"I have to work," I lie.

"Where?"

"Val's Bait and Thrift."

Dirk scowls. "Oh man, she's crazy. I once saw her scream at a guy in the parking lot of SuperValu just because he slapped his kid. I thought she was going to rip his eyes out."

My jaw tightens. "People shouldn't hit their kids."

"It's not her business."

I pull my hand back. "Isn't it? The kid sure as hell couldn't protect himself." Kicking aside the garbage at my feet, I press my face against the cold window. Pine branches bend under the heavy blanket of snow.

Dirk asks, "Why are you so worked up?"

"Take me home."

"Seriously? Come on. Just because I said one bad thing about Val? I'm sorry, alright?"

"We have nothing in common."

"Aw, we have tons."

"Like what?"

He thumps his fingers on the worn, discolored steering wheel, thinking. "Well, for starters, we both hate Ariana Grande."

I try to hide a smile, returning my gaze out the window. Outside, the wind has picked up, forcing snow from branches.

"Come on. Don't be mad." He says, "You're different from the other girls here and I like that."

My phone dings. There's a text from Maddy: "Love the pic of your short hair. You rock it! Sorry I couldn't get back to you last night. Brody and I went to a movie in Bemidji and didn't get back until late." There was the winking face emoji.

Is there an emoji that would fit this particular situation? Like one where I'm slitting my throat and dissolving into a puddle of blood?

I return my upward palm to the seat between us. Dirk promptly takes it.

We continue driving as the road twists further away from Raven Creek.

"There's beer in back under the blanket," he says. "Grab us a couple."

I reach back for two cans of Coors Light. I hand one to him and crack one for myself.

The beer goes down easily and fast.

"Right on," Dirk says. "Don't be shy."

I reach back for another.

We talk very little as we drink and drive further out of town. The roads look the same on the endless horizon. Trees, now sparser, separate fields that lay bare under the suffocating snow. Crows perch on electrical wires, branches and fence posts.

I finish the second beer and toss the can on the floor.

Dirk turns down a side road. There are no houses or other cars. He pulls over onto the gravel shoulder and parks. Turning to me, he smiles. "You look cold. Maybe I can warm you up?"

Putting his arm around my shoulder, he pulls me close and begins kissing me.

I gag on his overactive tongue, apologize and wait his incoming kiss with closed eyes. While I'm ready for his tongue, I'm not ready for his hand creeping up my back, then circling toward my breast. I block his hand with my elbow. As Dirk's roving hand retreats, his tongue hits overdrive.

Twenty-Three

DIRK MAKES IT CLEAR to everyone that I'm his girlfriend. He insists on taking my hand in the halls between classes. Even though his grip is too tight at times and his palm sweaty, I don't pull away.

Dirk's kissed me a few times at my locker as Brody passed by and, I'm not going to lie, the kiss got sweeter as Brody's disapproving gaze lingered. There's no love lost between Dirk and Brody, although I don't know the reason. Even Maddy, who knows nearly everything about everyone, is clueless.

I told Dirk I couldn't watch his wrestling match after school today because I have to work. It's a lie, but I stop at the Bait and Thrift anyway.

The sun shines after a record number of cloudy days in January. When I reach the store and push open the door, Val's sweeping the air with a thin, short wooden stick. Her hair is braided down her back and tied with a violet ribbon matching her flowery top.

Shutting the door, I say, "What are you doing?"

"Cleansing." She twirls. Smoke trails, then dissipates. "It's Palo Santo. A very powerful holy wood. It wards off evil and invites love and goodness."

I take off my coat, hang it on the hook and lean against the counter.

"Do you have a wand too?"

Val places the stick in the turquoise ceramic bowl near

the register. "Mock me all you want. You might not believe, but you can still benefit. I smudged your house when I cleaned it up before your mom came home."

"See how that worked?"

"With your dad back, your place will need more cleansing. I'll send a pack of Palo Santo sticks with you and a lighter. Go room to room and smudge, especially your folks' bedroom and the kitchen. Don't forget your room too."

"Maybe we can all pretend the magical smoke will change the sad reality of my sucky life."

"Sacred wood, blessings, affirmations and prayers of healing and strength help me see the good in people." Val sandwiches my hands between her warm ones. "You might think this is all whoo-hoo nonsense but, it's a helluva lot better than swimming in a cesspool of anger, despair and self-pity. We do what we can to give us strength to face each day. To survive."

"I'm surviving by staying as far away from Dad as I can until his trial next week."

The deep lines framing Val's dark eyes soften. "Honey, if you think your dad will be gone in a week and your life will be full of sunshine and roses, I hate to break it to you: The system ain't fair. At least it hasn't been for most women I know."

My throat feels like it's closing up. "I really don't want to talk about this right now."

"Then tell me about Dirk and you. I'm gone a weekend and you go and get yourself a boyfriend?"

My mouth falls open.

"You think I don't know things?"

"Did Brody tell you?"

"Young men don't tell old ladies things of the heart. No, I got that juicy news from Mrs. Winkelman. She's seen you holding hands in the hall at school. News travels fast from the high school to the grocery store in Raven Creek."

I groan. "I'm glad you find my social life entertaining."

"There's nothing wrong with a little lust. Now, love, that's scarier."

"I wouldn't call it anything."

"Maybe you could bring him by here so I can check him out?"

"That's not happening."

"Shame. I'll just have to scope him out with my higher powers."

I roll my eyes. "You're not psychic."

Val's smile teases me. "You're so sure?"

"Then tell me what grade I'm going to get on my stats test."

"Just because you don't see doesn't mean it can't be seen."

I mutter under my breath, "And you wonder why people think you're crazy?"

Val glares at me. "Who says I'm crazy?"

"Nobody."

"Now you're a liar?"

"I didn't mean it."

Val snatches the half-burned Palo Santo stick from my hand. "Go. Get out of my sight." She retreats into the back room through the dangling beads, leaving me alone with regret.

The house is quiet when I get home around four o'clock. Mom's note on the kitchen table says she and Zinnia are getting groceries.

The thought of having the house to myself is the best part of a miserable day. That sweet moment evaporates when I hear the front door open and Dad stomp snow from his steel toe boots on the entry rug. He's still wearing his coat when he pushes the kitchen door open. He takes the note in my hand. Everything is his to have and know.

He looks at me, as if trying to decide something. "This is as good as any time for your first driving lesson." Striding to the refrigerator, he retrieves two cans of Budweiser. His departing words: "Get your ass moving."

Dad's in the passenger seat of the pickup talking on his phone when I go outside. I've never been in his new truck. It's an armored tank compared to Mom's beat up Ford Focus.

"I got to go, Jags. Talk soon." He places the phone in a cupholder. He points out that I don't need a key; I only have to push the button. As soon as I do, the dashboard illuminates. The temperature display reveals -5 degrees Fahrenheit. A rock song blares from the speakers.

"Put it in drive and press on the gas with your right foot."

I feel paralyzed, my hands frozen on the wheel. The charcoal leather interior smells new.

"Any day now," Dad barks as he turns the music down.

The muscles across my shoulders and upper back tighten. The truck lurches forward when I put it in gear and press on the gas.

"Jesus. Not that hard. Ease into it and head toward Main Street, then out of town toward the reservation. There's not as many cars to hit." He looks at his watch. "Don't take all day. I got business with Jags."

"What kind?"

"None of your business," he snarls.

We haven't passed another car since we left town. Towering pines partially obscure the scattered trailer homes and abandoned machinery. Dirty, windswept snowbanks border the road.

Dad cracks a Budweiser and takes a gulp. He wipes his mouth, then points at the road. "Watch that rut."

I steer the truck to the left, narrowly missing it. The low sun slips behind a cloud.

"This place sucks," I say.

He looks out the window at nothing in particular. "Hell, when I was a kid, I spent too much time on these streets."

Mom and he attended high school in a suburb west of Minneapolis. This is the first time I heard he lived somewhere else. He never talked about his parents who died before I was born.

I say, "Is that why we moved here?"

"Nostalgic sentiment didn't bring me back. Far from it. We moved here because of a business opportunity." He's about to take a drink, but then bellows, "For Christ's sake, keep your eyes on the damn road and hold the wheel steady!"

I white knuckle the wheel, my gaze on the endless road ahead.

"Who'd you live with?"

"Different people." His voice is flat.

I hunch forward, increasing my grip on the steering wheel. The wind gusts, tossing light snow onto the windshield. I search for the wiper button.

"God dammit, pay attention and slow down! All it would take is an icy patch and we'd end up in the ditch."

"I wasn't going that fast."

"If I say you were going too fast, you were." He crushes the empty beer can and tosses it out the window. "Are you this pig-headed at school?"

"What do my teachers say at conferences? Oh, that's

right. You've never been to conferences." I clamp my jaw shut.

"They wouldn't tell me nothing I don't already know." He sneers, "Like you got your mom's stellar personality."

I tighten my hold on the wheel. "You married her. There must have been something you liked about her then."

"We were young and stupid."

"You didn't have to get married."

"St. Rita, your holier-than-thou grandmother, sure as hell thought we did. We had nothing, including the option of not relying on her manipulative generosity. Such a bitch."

"I can't see you doing anything you didn't want to do."

"Your mom was better looking then and not as clingy."

"I'm never getting married."

Dad's hands lurch toward the dash. "For the love of God, slow down. You're going to kill us," he says. "Pull over. I'm driving."

The seat belt engages when I stop too abruptly. Dad curses. I get out of the driver's seat, giving Dad a wide berth as I walk around the rear of the truck to get into the passenger seat.

I stare out at the barren January landscape as Dad drives toward home. The headlights expose towering wood poles connecting saggy wires. The sun begins its descent on the horizon.

Mom sits at the kitchen table wearing a thick, oversized University of Minnesota sweatshirt when Dad drops me off. Her hair is pulled back in a French braid, which makes her face look thin. She's not wearing any make-up.

"You were with Dad?"

"Yeah, we had some real quality father-daughter bonding time." I take off my jacket and toss it onto the chair.

"Is he coming back soon?"

"No idea. Why don't you call and ask him?"

She looks out the window at the dark sky. "He doesn't like me calling when he's got a lot on his mind." Lighting a cigarette, Mom inhales deeply, then releases smoke toward the ceiling.

A pan of Stouffer's lasagna sits on the cooktop. I lift the tinfoil lid, which is tented. One piece is missing; the remnants are on a paper plate near the sink. I know it's Zinnia's because there are chocolate sprinkles on it, her newest obsession. Taking a plate from the cupboard, I cut myself a piece, avoiding the burnt edges and I sit across from Mom without bothering to heat it up.

Mom pushes aside a loose hair that has fallen in her bloodshot eyes. There's a bruise on her wrist. Our eyes meet. She pulls the sweatshirt sleeve down.

"It's nothing," Mom says. "He doesn't like me asking so many questions. Sometimes I don't know when to stop. He has so much on his mind with the trial coming up."

Zinnia's feet skitter across the floor overhead.

"It can't come soon enough." I say, shoving a piece of cold lasagna into my mouth.

"You have to stop blaming him, Bridget. We need him."

I shove the plate aside. "I don't need him and neither do you. We'd be fine. I could get a different job, maybe two. Val might know of one for you."

"It's not that easy."

"What is harder than this?"

"It's complicated."

"If Grandma Rita knew what happened, she'd let us

move in with her. I know she would. You should have let me call her."

Mom snuffs out the cigarette and lights another. "Yeah, well I can't deal with her telling me, 'I told you so.' Not again."

The living room is all mine after Zinnia's finally asleep and Mom decides to wait for Dad in their bedroom. The TV volume is low as I study for a pre-calc test.

Knocking on the front door startles me. It gets louder and more urgent as I free myself from the afghan wrapped around my legs. When I open the door, Jags stands there in the same dirty "AJ's Taxidermy" hat he always wears.

"Hey, Bridget," he says, slow and sugary, "Your old man here?"

"Nope."

Jags steadies himself by holding onto the door frame.

"We were supposed to meet up and, well, I got delayed and all." He smirks and winks at me like I'm supposed to get an inside joke. "I called him but he hasn't picked up or answered my texts."

"I'll tell him you stopped."

Jags wedges his foot between the door and frame as I begin shutting the door. "How about I come in and wait for him?"

"He doesn't like people in the house when he's gone."

"It's colder than a well digger's ass. Come on, my balls are going to fall off soon. Besides, don't you think it'll piss off your old man if I'm not here like I said I'd be?"

Reluctantly, I open the door. Jags staggers inside and surveys the living room.

"It's a school night and I have a test, so feel free to watch TV if you want, but I'm going upstairs to study."

"Aw, come on, that's not very hospitable. You could at least offer me something to drink."

"Water or milk?"

Jags laughs. "Good one. Something stronger would be fine."

"That's what we got. Oh, and orange juice."

Jags pulls a flask from his camo hunting coat. "I guess it's BYOB." He takes a swig and offers it to me.

"No thanks. Test tomorrow."

He cocks his head. "You look different with your hair chopped off."

He creeps closer. Raising a hand, he brushes my bangs aside. "The hair's kinda butch, but at least you got a good face. I'm sure you can smile pretty when you want to."

I turn away so I don't have to look into his bloodshot eyes.

"My mom's putting Zinnia to bed," I lie. "She'll be down in a minute if you want to talk to her."

"Awfully late for little Z to be hitting the hay." His face draws closer and his hand lingers behind my ear. "Aren't you cute as a bug's ear," he whispers. His breath reeks of whiskey.

I swipe his hand away.

"A feisty girl," he says. "I like that."

"You need to go."

"I'm just giving you a compliment. Don't girls like that?"

"My dad wouldn't like it that you're here."

His cell phone rings. "Speak of the devil." Without taking his eyes off me, he answers it. "Bro, I'm at your house." He winks at me. "Yeah, I can meet you there in five."

Jags shoves his phone into the side pocket of his jacket.

"Sadly, our time together must end." Before I know it, he's coming in for a kiss. There's no way to avoid his hard pressed lips against mine and his tongue snaking into my mouth.

I gag, which makes him laugh.

"Happy studying, sweet thing." He swats my butt and staggers out the door.

A mouthful of Ivory soap couldn't remove the vile taste.

Twenty-Four

"DIRK'S MAD YOU WON'T GO to the winter dance tomorrow," Maddy says, as I sit on her bed after school while she models dresses. "He wants his girlfriend there. Don't you think that seems reasonable?"

"Except I detest dances," I moan without sharing I've never exactly been to a dance.

This week we've been encouraged to show school spirit by wearing clothes to match the theme-of-the-day. I've chosen to wear the clothes I always wear: jeans and oversized sweatshirts.

Maddy models a short black dress with an open, low back. She critiques herself from different angles in the full length mirror affixed to the bedroom door. "Do you like this or the cream one?"

"You look great in either."

My fingers caress the satin trim of a long-sleeved, navy blue dress that Maddy dismissively flung aside.

"Change your mind about going to the dance. It'll be fun. Go ahead and try on the dress."

Reluctantly, I retreat to the bathroom off Maddy's room. It's nicer than anything I've ever owned. After slipping my hands through the sleeves, the slinky material glides over my hips.

Maddy hollers, "How's it fitting? Are you going to model it for me? There's this other black dress you could try if that one doesn't work."

The dress falls loosely, brushing the top of my knees and dipping slightly in front to reveal some, but not too much, cleavage. As I twirl, the air lifts the fabric from my skin.

Maddy knocks and then pushes open the door. "The dress looks amazing on you. Wait here while I go get shoes."

I remember poring over Grandma Rita's albums with the pictures of Mom in fancy dresses, posing with her friends before high school dances.

Where are all of Mom's friends now?

Maddy returns with an armful of shoes, which she deposits at my feet.

"Thanks, but there's no need to try them on," I say, lifting the dress over my head, I hurry and throw my sweatshirt back. "Dad won't let me go."

Maddy follows me back to her room and sits next to me on the bed. "That sucks. All you ever do is take care of Zinnia and your mom, go to school, or work. You need a life too. And some fun. You're getting cranky."

"Dad's got court on Monday and things are tense at home."

"All the more reason for you to have fun at the dance and stay over. Get away from it for a night. Besides, it'll fix things with you and Dirk."

I roll my eyes. "I've got other things to worry about other than Dirk." I hug one of the decorative pillows with lace trim against my chest and sink against the King-sized, goose down pillows atop the floral duvet. "It's just overwhelming at times, you know? I'm afraid he'll get off and Mom's freaking out that he'll serve time."

Maddy moves closer, draping her arms around my shoulders.

I can't remember when someone, other than Dirk, Mom or Zinnia was this close to me. Her touch makes me feel uncomfortable.

"How about I drop you off and ask permission for you to come to the dance and sleepover? I'll pledge to take exquisite care of you," Maddy says. "Girl Scout promise. Cross my heart. Whatever it takes. Your mom could come take pictures with the other moms. It'll be fun."

I laugh. "Fine, but I think I can manage the ask on my own."

The thought of having my own pictures with friends in fancy dresses smiling and having fun convinces me, despite my better judgement.

The living room is dark when Maddy drops me off at home. Zinnia is sprawled on the couch watching TV. I fling my coat and backpack on the recliner.

"Where's Mom?"

Without taking her thumb out of her mouth, Zinnia mutters, "Upstairs."

"Dad?"

She shrugs.

Mounting the stairs, I call Mom's name. She's not in her bedroom where dirty clothes cover the hardwood floor surrounding the unmade bed. The hall bathroom door is closed. I knock once. No answer. My hand turns the silver knob.

Mom crouches, naked, over the toilet.

I yank a towel from the hook on the back of the door and drape it over Mom's shoulders. She sits back on her legs and wipes her mouth with the corner of the towel that doesn't fully cover her small breasts. Her foot hits a thin piece of white plastic, which slides across the floor. Picking it up, I see a window with two lines: Mom's pregnant.

"Does Dad know?"

Mom shakes her head and closes her eyes.

My fingers dip into the cold bath water. When I was little, Mom and I bathed together. We'd make big, sudsy hairdos and mustaches with the pink bubble bath she got at the Dollar Store. Our splashing drenched the floor. Afterwards, Mom wrapped me in the fluffy towel and brushed my hair.

"Where's Dad?"

"Fargo. He'll be back on Sunday."

"When are you going to tell him?"

Mom curls her body into her bent knees. "When I have to."

I release the tub drain.

"Tomorrow night I'm going to the winter dance with Maddy and sleeping over at her house. She has a dress I can wear."

I want a picture of myself smiling with friends, even if it's only one time and no one ever looks at it in an album.

"This can be another thing we don't tell Dad," I say.

Twenty-Five

MADDY AND I ARRIVE at the winter dance fashionably late. The prep work at Maddy's house took hours. You'd think Maddy had training as a professional model. First, she blew out my hair and used sticky product to mold it into place. After painstakingly painting my face, I couldn't tell Maddy I'd rather wash it all off and be recognizable. She, on the other hand, looks amazing. No surprise. Maddy's mom took pictures from every direction and angle. My face hurts from smiling.

As Maddy and I walk down the school's hallway lined with pink and green neon streamers, my feet already ache in the heels Maddy talked me into wearing.

In the gym, beneath the flashing strobe light, Mr. Anhorn is dressed in an orange polyester leisure suit. He's demonstrating the Hustle to the freshman volleyball suck-ups who actually took the 1970's theme seriously by wearing bell bottoms, big hair, and flowered tops. There was no way, Maddy said, we were going to waste the dresses her mom bought.

Maddy beelines toward Brody who's talking to his buddies in the back of the gym and Dirk swoops in. He's wearing jeans and a white shirt, which reveals too much of his pale bare chest. His arms encircle my waist. "You look hot."

Loud music plays to a mostly empty dance floor. Eventually, more people crowd into the stuffy gym. Sweat forms between my breasts and on my brow. My hair wilts under the weight of the hair product Maddy applied.

"I've got to go to the bathroom," I say.

When I emerge, Dirk saunters over to me with a cup of red punch. "You missed Nate slow dancing with his blow up date. Anhorn went apeshit and took it away when he started grinding it." He laughs. "It was great."

"Where's Maddy?"

Dirk withdraws a flask from his coat and pours clear liquid into his glass. "Don't know. Don't care."

I scan the crowd.

"You look amazing tonight," Dirk says. "You should wear dresses more often." He traces his finger down my exposed spine. "Maybe we should dance?"

"I'm thirsty," I say, barely avoiding his incoming mouth that reeks of Copenhagen and peppermint schnapps.

He dangles his cup with a coy smile.

"No thanks. I'll get my own."

Dirk's sweaty hand slides into my cold one. Tethered, we cross the gym in our own dance of pulling away and pulling back. The bowls of punch, pretzels, and M & M's are nearly empty. Dirk rubs my lower back as I sip Hawaiian punch.

When Dirk says he has to take a leak, I take the opportunity to go outside for fresh air.

Aimee is standing outside the main doors. Her long, straight black hair blends into the shadows. She's wearing a letter jacket over her short red dress and smoking a cigarette, which she tucks behind her back, until she sees it's only me.

Aimee glares at me through hard eyes lined with smeared mascara. "That friend of yours should keep her hands off what isn't hers."

"I don't know what you're talking about."

"Maddy started digging her claws into Brody as soon as Evan dumped her."

"Talk to her, not me."

A low riding car with thudding music passes the front of the school. An empty Busch Light beer can flies out the window and lands near the snowbank.

Aimee discards the glowing butt and squashes it with her heel. "You think you're pretty hot stuff, don't you?" Her stare could melt the lake's thick ice. For a moment I wonder if she's going to hit me.

"I've got to get back in."

"Yeah, you don't want to be seen talking to me."

"What's your deal?"

Aimee narrows her dark, almond-shaped eyes. "I got no deal. But, tell me, what's the deal with your dad and Jags?" Silky hair falls across Aimee's high cheekbones, which she tucks behind her ear. "I see him hanging around in that fancy truck with Jags all buddy-buddy."

Aimee obviously enjoys taunting me. I refuse to give her any such satisfaction. "I'll tell Maddy and Brody you say hey—unless they've already left to do whatever they might be doing."

It strikes a chord with Aimee who looks like she wants to say something, but I turn and go back inside before she can utter another word.

Maddy finally shows up a half hour later in her long winter coat. She looks pissed. Dirk sulks away when I say Maddy and I need to talk.

"Where you been?"

"Brody and I went for a drive," she says, flinging her coat onto the bleachers. "Now, he's gone with Aimee." She sneers, "I told him there's nothing he can do, but he won't listen to me. He said he didn't want me coming with him because it would make things worse."

"What are you're talking about?"

"Her younger sister's taken off again. I told him she'd eventually show up and there's nothing he can do. But, he insists he has to help Aimee even though they're not dating anymore."

The music stops and the overhead lights pop on. As my eyes adjust, I look down at my feet squeezed into shoes I didn't want to wear and fingernails painted with sparkling red polish that's already chipping off.

I say, "Can we go back to your place? Preferably before Dirk returns?"

"Yeah, I don't feel in the mood for the after parties. They sound lame."

As I'm putting on my coat, Maddy shoves her phone towards my nose. "Look at the picture of us I posted on Instagram." We look like the best of friends with our faces close and our smiles bright. Over 200 people had already liked and commented on the picture.

Maddy drops me off at home around noon on Sunday. Dad's truck is still gone while Mom's car is buried under a mound of new snow.

Mom sits at the kitchen table cradling her coffee mug. The house is quiet except for the dripping faucet. Mom's eyes brighten when she sees me. "Did you have a good time?"

I step over Zinnia's crayons and coloring book scattered on the floor near Mom's feet. A plate of cold bacon and blueberry pancakes is untouched on the counter.

"It was okay,"

She's eager for details I don't want to give.

"Anyone ask you to dance?"

I tear off a piece of cold, rubbery pancake. "Not really."

Her smile fades. "Oh, I'm sorry."

"Why?"

"Well, it's nice to be asked."

I shrug. "If you want to dance."

"I always liked being asked."

"Clearly, I'm not you," I say.

"Well, it was nice of Maddy's mom to let you get ready there."

"Yeah, she's the best."

"I wish you would have let me do your make-up or nails." Mom forces a smile. "Did anyone take pictures?"

"No," I lie and push the plate away.

Twenty-six

ON MONDAY, Dad paces the living room in a suit Jags loaned him. Val coordinated my outfit, which she said would look mature and enhance my credibility with the court: a pair of black dress pants, a boring blouse my grandma wouldn't wear, and a short-waisted black jacket to cover it.

Dad hollers up the stairs, "Ashley, you don't have to take all God damned day. For Christ's sake, I'm supposed to be at the courthouse in twenty minutes."

Nowhere in Raven Creek is more than five minutes away.

Dad turns to me. "Remember, they'll try to trick you. Get you to say things to help them, not us."

He gave me a script, should I be called to the stand, but I rehearsed my own statement. Not his words. Not his version.

Mom's high heels click down the uncarpeted stairs. She's wearing the dull beige dress Dad chose for her. When she's barely at the landing, he tosses her coat to her and storms out.

Mom struggles to zip the coat. Her fingers are shaking. As I try dislodging the fabric trapped in the zipper's teeth, Mom leans her head against mine.

Dad lays on the horn.

No one talks during the short drive to the courthouse. The sky meets the windswept, dirty snow. Rather than waiting at Raven Creek's only traffic light when there are no other cars, Dad glides through.

Flags hang limp on the pole in front of the courthouse, a three-story, boxy stone building on Main Street. After parking, Dad walks ahead on the salt smattered sidewalk. Mom's arm links with mine as we follow.

We take the stairs, rather than the elevator, to the assigned courtroom. A scrawny man with a pencil mustache struts toward us. He ushers Dad into a small conference room and directs Mom and me inside to wait.

We push open the thick, heavy doors. The courtroom is empty and musty. There are no windows, only round ceiling lights. In front, there's a polished mahogany bench with a high back leather chair for the judge. The witness stand is next to the bench. The jury box is along the wall. Chairs flank two rectangular tables facing the judge's bench.

Mom and I stand behind the wood rail partitioning us off from the area for the judge, jury, witnesses and attorneys. Are we supposed to sit in the front or back? Which side? Will Dad come back and sit with us or do we sit alone? We decide to sit in the third row of benches on the left side of the divided aisle toward the middle.

A balding man with round glasses and a barrel belly barges through the door behind the bench carrying a stack of folders. He arranges the folders on the judge's desk. A woman follows and sits on a chair in front of a machine with keys. She waves to a sheriff who enters and positions himself off to the side of the courtroom. They make small talk about climate change not impacting the thickness of the ice on area lakes.

We wait alone in our row. Mom frequently cranes her neck, searching for Dad.

Val squeezes her face between Mom and me and whispers with her coffee breath, "You two holding up?" Mom smiles weakly with her hands clasped in her lap. I say nothing. Val pats my shoulder like a dog, then sits back in her row.

I pick the cuticle of my thumb, exposing raw skin. Sucking the side of the thumb, I taste blood. Mom takes my hand with her sweaty palm. I resort to counting the ceiling tiles.

Eventually, Dad enters the courtroom and sits next to Mom. She exchanges my hand for his. He whispers something that I can't hear, then joins his attorney at the table facing the judge's bench.

The courtroom door creaks open. I turn and see Jags as he slinks into the back row.

The balding man with the bulging gut returns. He's followed by a distinguished looking woman in a black robe. We're told to rise for the Honorable Jill Eichenberry as court is now in session. The judge strikes the gavel and tells us to sit down.

When the case State v. Reid is called, Dad rises along with his public defender.

"In the matter of the State v. Reid," Judge Eichenberry says, "it's my understanding a plea agreement has been reached. Is that correct?"

A woman stands and identifies herself as the County Attorney, Peg Downey. "Yes. The State has agreed to drop the charge of Felony Domestic Assault in exchange for Gross Misdemeanor Domestic Assault."

"Is that correct, counsel?"

Dad's attorney responds, "Yes, your Honor."

"The extent of injuries and pictures of the victim from December 6th, are disturbing to say the least," Judge Eichenberry says. "There are also three prior domestic violence-related convictions in less than ten years."

"Your Honor, the victim has recovered and consents to the plea agreement." Dad's attorney turns and points at us. I stare at the floor that is dirty from boots and shoes carrying in the winter slush and salt. He continues, "In fact, she never wanted charges pursued in the first place."

Judge Eichenberry purses her lips. Her glare is swift and piercing. "Counsel, the justice system is designed to hold people accountable even if victims do not wish it." She sighs, looking one more time at the file. "But, I appreciate that going through a trial can be difficult for all parties. Therefore, I will accept the plea. Swear him in."

Dad raises his hand and swears to tell the truth. He states his name and address.

"Mr. Reid," Judge Eichenberry states, "do you understand that you are pleading guilty to the lesser charge of gross misdemeanor domestic assault and consent?"

That's it? He's not going to have to pay for almost killing Mom? No attempted murder? Just another domestic assault to add to his record?

Dad stands tall. "Yes, your Honor."

I squeeze my fists, hidden in the pockets of my jacket, until my fingers, like my body, feel numb. I don't hear the rest of what Dad admits or agrees to.

Judge Eichenberry concludes the matter, putting the closed file aside. "The clerk will set the sentencing date after the pre-sentence investigation is complete."

That investigation won't mention the birthday parties or sleepovers I never had because he might come home drunk or make a scene. It won't talk about Zinnia crying herself to sleep or clinging to me so tightly my arm goes numb. And, it won't say how much I wish he was dead.

We leave the courtroom in search of Dad and find him talking to Jags at the end of a hall on the first floor where we came in.

Val says, "I gotta use the ladies' room." She casts a disdainful glance toward Dad and Jags and leaves.

Mom and I wait with our coats on near the main entrance. With each person coming or going, the wind gusts and displaces Mom's perfect hair. She smiles politely even though there's no recognition or connection with the strangers.

Dad faces Jags and doesn't see us. But, Jags does. When he points in our direction, Dad doesn't turn to face us; instead, his hands dramatically shoot toward the ceiling. Jags' face grows serious. Then, he nods and hands Dad an envelope. They fist bump and Jags leaves.

Rage shadows Dad's face as he approaches us. "The clerk set a sentencing date for six weeks. Jags and I are going to Fargo. I've got business to take care of."

"Now?" Mom strokes Dad's arm with a sweet look. "Can't you do it later?"

Dad swipes her hand away and sneers, "Jesus Christ. You'd think you'd lay off for one God damned minute."

"Carter, I just thought it'd be nice to go to the cafe and talk. Just the three of us."

"I don't need this shit right now." His raised voice causes the elderly couple sitting on the nearby bench to suspend their conversation. They draw their staring faces closer and whisper.

"You think I got time to talk? You're not the one whose ass might be sent away for a year. But, maybe you'd like that."

Mom recoils as if he smacked her.

I'm relieved to see Val returning from the restroom. She stops and feigns invisibility near the water fountain, which would be easier if she wasn't wearing a purple wool cape with multi-colored fringe.

Dad shoots a contemptuous look toward Val. "Have her take you home." Then, he bolts out.

Val strides over and wraps her arm around Mom's drooping shoulders. "It's alright, honey. You both come to my house and I'll get you a nice meal and we'll talk."

Mom casts her eyes toward the floor. "It would have been nice to celebrate together as a family."

I say, "What exactly are we celebrating? That he's going to get off easy for what he did? That you didn't die so all is good?"

Mom ignores me and walks toward the door.

I yell, "Go ahead, walk away. Chase after Dad. You don't worry about anyone but him. That's what you do."

Mom turns and faces me. Tears streak her mascara.

I ignore Mom's eyes imploring me to stop. "What about us? What about that baby you're so good at hiding? Don't we matter at all to you? Or, just him?"

Color drains from Mom's face. She looks like she might topple over from the weight of my words.

Val mutters under her breath with thick sarcasm, "Well, isn't that just great. Another baby."

Twenty-seven

RAISED VOICES invade my dreamless sleep. Zinnia cries out and kicks off the covers. Grasping in the dark, my hands search until I find her well-loved bunny wedged between us. I rub Zinnia's cheek with its velvety ear.

"Mr. Hoppy wants to snuggle," I say.

Zinnia's breathing settles as I stroke her wavy hair. She whispers, "His ear's wet."

"That's because you were crying and his ear was your blanket."

"I wasn't crying."

"You were," I say. "In your sleep."

"I don't remember crying."

"Shh. Roll over. I'll rub your back."

"Draw a picture and let me guess."

"Try and go back to sleep."

I circle my fingers on her thin, princess nightgown.

"Is it a flower?"

"Go to sleep."

"It feels like a flower. Maybe a tree."

"Sleep."

It's hard to block out the yelling downstairs. Dad wasn't home from his two-day road trip with Jags when I fell asleep. Mom was beside herself with each passing hour that Dad was gone despite Val's assurances he'd be back. "They always are," she reminded Mom.

"Bri?"

"Yeah."

"The yelling hurts my tummy."

I move closer. "Let's play a game. I'll draw letters and you try to guess."

The moonlight casts a silverly glow in the room.

Zinnia whispers, "Do you think Daddy will go away again?"

"Close your eyes," I whisper. Her nightgown is too thin. I pull the comforter higher, over her shoulders. "What letter did I draw?"

She pauses. "Z?"

"Good. What's this one?"

"I. Are you doing my name?"

"Aren't you smart? Now, close your eyes and sleep. I'm tired and have a test tomorrow morning." I rest my arm on her back. "Don't let the bed bugs bite."

She answers on cue, "If they do, hit them with a shoe with all your might."

"Night, night, Z."

I kiss the top of her head.

Zinnia startles. "Did you hear that?"

"It's nothing, just the wind," I say, rubbing her back again.

"Is Mom okay?"

"She's fine."

"How do you know?"

In a deep, low voice I say theatrically, "I have magical powers and know everything."

Zinnia snuggles closer. "What if it's not the wind?"

I stroke her hair. "It is."

She looks up at me. "How come you're not afraid?"

"Trust me. My magical powers will protect you." And, while I don't believe it, she does.

I lay awake listening to the raised voices downstairs.

Eventually, Zinnia falls asleep. I extricate my arm, which has fallen asleep under the weight of her head. Her eyes flutter open briefly, then she finds her thumb. I tuck Mr. Hoppy close to her chest. When I'm finally satisfied that Zinnia is sleeping soundly, my hand searches, and finds, Dad's bottle of Jim Beam that I've stashed under the bed.

I found the bottle in a box when I was looking for my collection of Harry Potter books in the basement. I planned to flush it down the toilet. But, I tried a few swigs one night when I couldn't bear all the yelling and crying. The amber liquid warmed my throat and I fell asleep and was comatose until morning. It was a magic elixir blocking all consciousness.

While Zinnia clutches Mr. Hoppy, her thumb resting at the curve of her mouth, I take a sip. Zinnia's soft snores, more like a purr, distract from the yelling downstairs. I brush aside a strand of Zinnia's golden hair that has fallen onto her flushed cheek and hug the cool glass bottle close to my chest. The wind howls. I take another drink. This one longer. It smells like licorice or cinnamon, I can't tell which, but it glides down easily. My insides feel warm as I return the bottle to its hiding place.

Twenty-Eight

PERSISTENT POUNDING on the front door wakes me. I'm alone in bed and its nearly noon. My head pounds after another self-numbing rendezvous with Mr. Beam. Tossing on the overworn sweatshirt that Emma gave me, I plod down the hallway toward the stairs. I stop when I hear voices.

Jerry, the officer present on the evening of Dad's arrest in December, stands wide-legged in our front entrance talking to Mom. "You're certain, Mrs. Reid, that you don't know where he is?"

"I told you, I don't."

"When did you last see him?"

"He went out two nights ago and didn't come back."

His face is serious. "The timing is curious, wouldn't you agree? He disappears on the day that he's going to be sentenced?" Jerry pauses, without losing eye contact with Mom, and says, "We recovered his truck in the ditch near the railroad tracks south of Raven Creek. It was covered in eight inches of snow but there were no keys and it was unlocked. Seems odd, doesn't it? That he disappears like that?"

Mom responds with silence.

Jerry runs his thick knuckled hands through his silver mop of hair. "Did he tell you where he was going, what he was doing, or who he was with?"

Mom shifts her gaze to the floor and shakes her head. "He doesn't tell me everything."

"Any idea?"

"No."

"Not a text or a call of any kind since he left?"

Mom shakes her head and hugs her arms tight to her body, rocking slightly.

"That didn't concern you?"

She glares at the officer. "I'm always concerned about him."

Jerry scans the room. "So, he's not here?"

Mom sweeps her arm wide, motioning toward the living room and kitchen. "Look for yourself if you don't believe me."

Jerry flips through a notebook. "I haven't been able to verify his current employer."

"He used to work at the grain elevator, but now he helps Jags."

"Al Jaegers at AJ's Taxidermy?"

Mom nods.

"Your husband's a taxidermist?"

"No."

"What exactly does your husband help Jags with?"

"We don't talk about work."

"Have they known each other long?"

"I don't know."

Jerry fondles the extra folds of skin on his neck while staring at Mom over the top of his bifocal glasses. "If you know where he is, you need to tell me. There's a warrant out for his arrest."

Mom says softly, "Don't you think I'd like to know where my husband is?"

Jerry closes the notebook. "Contact us if you find out where he is." Seeing me perched on the top stair, he says, "Do you know anything?"

"No," I say.

He doesn't press me. He replaces his hat and walks out.

In the living room, Mom is barely able to catch her breath. I wrap my arms around her and she leans her head on my shoulder.

"He didn't take clothes or anything so he has to be coming back, right?"

I stroke her hair. "Have you tried calling him?"

"It goes right into voicemail." Her chest heaves with sobs.

We sit, left alone together in a town most people drive through, knowing nothing about why Dad abandoned everything, including his prized truck.

Twenty-Nine

THE ONLY CONSTANT in my life in the last two weeks since Dad's disappearance is working at the Bait and Thrift and the relentless texts from Dirk about hanging out because he misses me.

The last thing I need is another person needing me.

Val's in the back of the store when I arrive today. Following the music, I stand behind the multi-colored beads hanging in the doorway and watch her sweeping the floor while singing along to the Rolling Stones' song, "Ain't Got No Satisfaction" (part of her favorite, repeating playlist). Her hair is loosely stacked on her head, held in place with a beaded headband.

I'm careful not to reveal my presence because she'd certainly try and get me to dance. It's what she does. Last week, she got Earl, a grumpy walleye fisherman, to dance with her when he came in to buy a bucket of minnows. Earl's protest was weaker than the week before. She's wearing him down. Val, like the unrelenting winter in northern Minnesota, does that.

When the playlist shuffles to Bob Dylan's "Forever Young," Val sways to the music, her feet rooted to the floor. Then, she stops and closes her eyes. She stands stone still.

I push through the beads and go to her. "You okay?"

She cringes and nods. Her chest heaves.

"What's wrong?"

"Not a damn thing," she snaps. "Why does there have to be anything wrong?"

"It's just . . ."

Val waves her hand at me like she's shooing a fly. Her skin is pale and slack.

"You don't look fine."

Val avoids my eyes. "Well, I am, thank you very much. I don't need you fussing at me. I'm just an old lady who can't move like she used to," she says, standing more upright.

Val doesn't object when I guide her to the metal folding chair. She leans forward, forearms resting on her thick thighs.

She finally opens her eyes.

"You okay?"

"Don't worry about me," Val says, smiling weakly. "I'm fine. How's your mom?"

"She's in bed a lot."

"Throwing up still?"

"Yeah, and she says she's bleeding some."

The lines on Val's weathered face deepen as she frowns. "Laying on her left side?"

"I have no idea."

"There's some herbs that'll help bleeding."

Val starts coughing again. She's sweating and her skin is flushed. When she stops and catches her breath, she retrieves a tissue from the designated storage center between her expansive breasts, and dabs the perspiration on her forehead.

I grab a coffee mug, fill it with tap water and hand it to her. She takes a sip.

Dirk texts me again. I tuck my phone into my back pocket without responding.

"Are you sure you're okay?"

She nods and closes her eyes.

I wait silently even though I have so many questions about what I should do to help her.

Val opens her eyes. "Remind me to tell your mom that the casino's hiring. I got a contact in HR and told him she'd fill out an application."

"Dad doesn't like her working."

"He's not here is he?" She's about to say something else, but doubles over with a coughing fit.

I hand the box of tissues to her.

Val spits something into the tissue. Before she can completely fold it over, I see the blood.

"You have to go to the doctor."

She shakes her head, clutching the tissue in her closed fist. "Not a damn thing they can do." Her eyes are bloodshot and tired.

"How do you know if you don't go to the doctor?"

"I'm just old. And, I smoke too much. What else they going to tell me? Stop smoking? I know that already. I don't need to give them any of my God damned money to hear what I already know."

"Why don't you quit then?"

"I do. Every week."

"Hopefully you don't keel over before you really quit."

"Well, Miss Smarty Pants, why don't you make yourself useful and organize and mark that box of new drop-offs while I balance the books in front."

Val rises slowly and retreats through the beads. Drumming music begins playing. I get a whiff of Palo Santo wood burning and hear Val coughing some more.

Dirk texts me: "Where you at?"

Maddy thinks I need to give him a chance. She says he's thick headed at times, and a bit wild, but he's a good guy deep down. Like everyone in Raven Creek, they've known each other forever. They were in the same kindergarten class and their mothers volunteer in the church nursery. She says he'll be crushed if I dump him. Funny, Maddy never considers how I'm feeling in this "relationship."

I'm debating my response when I hear a thud. Rushing into the store, I find Val on the floor behind the glass counter. The round plastic containers of wax worms are scattered on the floor.

I run to Val and roll her over. She groans. I stroke her colorless cheek. It feels like Silly Putty. Her eyes flutter open, then close. She tries to speak, but can't. Her body is heavy and limp in my arms. Tears sting my eyes as I reach for my phone and call 911.

Thirty

VAL CLASPS MY HAND during the ambulance ride to the Bemidji hospital. When they admit her, I learn Valerie Amber Smith turned 72 yesterday without telling anyone.

A pool-ball shaped nurse with wire-rimmed glasses and greasy hair hanging limp to her shoulders sits behind a desk, periodically calling people up and talking to them in a hushed tone. No one has come looking for me in the past two hours.

I send Mom a text, telling her only that I need to help Val and it could be late. I don't tell her why or where I'm at because two of us don't need to worry. I consider texting Brody, but quickly dismiss that idea. Val would go ballistic if I told anyone about this without her blessing. In any case, I don't know anything yet.

The air in the hospital's windowless, crowded waiting room is heavy and stale. Thick black coffee, white Styrofoam cups, and powdered creamer are available at a station along the far wall. There are various end tables with shaded lamps and magazines no one reads. Some people stare into space like zombies, but most are constantly on their phones. Waiting, I can see Val's eyes looking back at me as they whisked her to an examination room.

A dark framed picture hangs on the tan wall. The sun is rising over large trees bordering a field of harvested hay. The trees' leaves are varying shades of gold, orange and burnt red. An unsuspecting buck enters the field as an orange-clad man in a metal deer stand raises his rifle. Having watched

Bambi as a child, I know what comes next.

Dirk sends another text. He wants to hang out and wonders where I am at and what I'm doing. I don't reply, which only triggers a tirade. There's no escaping him. Not even here.

I finally muster enough courage to send him a cowardly text: "I don't want to be your girlfriend anymore. Sorry. It's not you. I've got too much going on right now." I feel a mixture of relief and guilt. Immediately, my phone rings. It's Dirk. I decline the call. The relief I feel from finally ending the relationship lifts some of the heaviness in my chest. I delete all of our messages back and forth and then block his number.

The nurse finally summons me to her desk. She says I can see Val, but offers no other information. She leads me back to a room on the far end of the hall next to the nurses' station. There are no windows. A dim light glows above the bed. Val lies on her back with her eyes closed. She's dressed in a faded blue and white hospital gown and covered with a thin cream blanket. Her hair hangs loose around her shoulders.

A different nurse enters the room with a pleasant smile and introduction: Alison. She accesses the computer by the bed with a plastic badge hooked to her uniform and punches something in. A bag of clear fluids, hanging on a pole beside the bed, empties into Val's veins through a thin tube taped to her right arm, which is propped on a pillow. Two small clear plastic prongs poke into Val's nostrils. Oxygen, I'm told. The nurse offers little in the way of an explanation about Val, only that she's resting comfortably, the doctor will be back to check on her at some point, and they are waiting to transfer her out of ER and upstairs to another room. She points out the call button on the bed by Val's hand before departing.

Val's rattling breath rises and falls. When I try coordinating my breath with hers, I can't. Hers is too fast. I reach for her warm, limp hand.

I gently stroke her thick, purplish veins.

Tears sting my eyes. With my free hand, I wipe them away.

Val squeezes my hand. "Aren't you a sight."

"How are you feeling?"

"Like shit."

"The nurse says the doctor will be back, but I'm not sure if it's before you go to your room."

"He's 12. What does he know?"

I scan the room. "Can I get you some water? I could also ask the nurse for food or whatever you want."

"I can't have what I want."

"I'm sure they'll make you better," I say.

Val's fingers wrap around mine. "Honey, that ain't gonna happen."

Her eyes hold mine.

"Sure it will. You probably need some medicine for that cough and you'll be back to your ornery old self." I force a laugh and squeeze her hand. "Just wait and see. I'll work more so you can rest. You don't even have to pay me."

She grimaces as she tries shifting in the bed. "That's not what I'm worried about."

The machine beeps, then stops. The numbers flash. I have no idea what any of them mean.

Val's eyes close.

My heart quickens. I lean closer. My face is inches from Val's weathered face. I whisper, "You okay? Should I call the nurse?"

She shakes her head and slowly licks her lips.

I move a strand of hair that fell forward, covering her finely painted black brow.

Val opens her eyes and smiles weakly. "I'm not doing chemo or radiation again," she says softly. "I'll let my time run out on my own terms. And, not in this God damned hospital."

Cancer?

There's no holding back the tears. My hand reaches back for the generic, rectangular tissue box on the narrow, fake wood table alongside the bed.

Val opens her arms as far as the tubes allow. I fold toward her soft, generous breasts. My whole body shakes from the inside out. I melt into her warm, open body. Val rubs my back, letting me cry. She smells like the lavender essential oil she uses in her homemade facial products, laundry detergent, and diffuser.

Val lifts my face towards her. "Bridget, we all die. We just don't know when." The lines around her black eyes are deep. "And," she says, "living's the hard part, not dying."

Thirty-One

"THE THRIFT NEEDS A FACELIFT," Val announces when she returns to work after a weeklong, doctor mandated rest at home that she declared unnecessary and worthless. "A fresh coat of paint is long overdue."

The hospital discharged Val after a day when she bullied the "Baby Doctor" to let her go, saying there wasn't a damn thing he could do to keep her there. She refused all treatment for the lung cancer. I haven't a clue about the time she's got left. She says she refuses to waste any energy on such thoughts. So, we both act like nothing is different.

"Brody's coming by soon," Val says.

"I can do whatever you need done. I don't need his help."

"You ain't the only one who needs money. Plus, the painting will go faster with the two of you."

When Brody arrives an hour later, Val waves her hands in front of her nose. "For God's sake, you couldn't shower first?"

He makes the dramatic gesture of sniffing his hairy armpits. "What's the big deal? It's a great day for a run." The end of March thankfully has brought teasing sunshine and warmer days.

Val scoffs. "You have to be in close proximity to other living beings."

Body odor, even on him, isn't sweet, but I've smelled worse.

Val tells us to follow her into the back area. The tables are piled high with tagged clothing and pushed into the center of the room. Only the yellowed tape that held the posters of Sting, Bon Jovi, Rod Stewart and Paul Simon remain on the dingy walls. There's a square, plastic laundry basket with brushes, rollers and paint trays. A tarp for covering the floor is folded and placed on top.

Brody pries open a gallon of paint with a flat screwdriver.

"You'll need to stir the paint first," Val says. He shoots her a look like he knew that.

Brody says, "You couldn't pick something neutral?"

Val hands me a stiff, wide brush. "Indigo's my favorite color." Her phone rings. She tells the person to hold on, reminds us to use the tarp and not to drip too much paint, and returns to the bait shop.

Brody unfolds the tarp and spreads it out along the far wall. We make small talk, but there's not much to say. Brody and I move to different parts of the same wall. I dip the brush into the paint, glide it on the wall, and pretend I'm concerned about perfection on an imperfect wall.

Val starts hacking in the bait shop. I stop painting, listening, until she stops.

A truck with a loud muffler pulls into the lot. A bell sounds. I recognize Earl's rough, deep voice. Val returns to the back, grabs her purse and digs out her lipstick. "I'm gonna run out for a bite to eat." She applies the red lipstick perfectly without a mirror and says with a wink on her way out, "Or, maybe something else."

The spring sun warms the room as we continue to roll and brush the paint over the uneven, patched walls. Brody paints with more precision than I, careful to create a straight line against the ceiling using a flat steel edger that he found in the bottom of the basket.

Brody dips his brush into the can, letting a stream of paint fall back into the can. "I can't believe it took you so long to ditch Dirk. You're too good for him."

"I don't know about that."

Brody says, "I do."

"Well, at least I was honest with him."

He puts the brush down. "What's that supposed to mean?"

"You give Maddy mixed messages."

"How exactly am I doing that?"

"Spending time with Aimee when you're supposed to be dating Maddy."

Brody's strokes become harsher, faster, and less precise. "Aimee and I have known each other since we were in first grade. I sure as hell ain't dumping her as my friend." The back of his t-shirt is drenched in sweat. "That's not who I am. And, right now, I'm about the only real friend she has."

We paint for a long time without speaking. A chain saw cuts the silence. The paint fumes give me a headache. The paint, a cross between grape jelly and the night sky at dusk, hides the dirty walls that I never noticed.

I don't want Brody to think I'm a total jerk so I ask, "How's Aimee's sister?"

He continues painting without a glance in my direction. "Alive."

The paint from my brush drips onto the tarp. "There's no way Aimee could have stopped her from running away from the sounds of it."

"Just because you can't stop someone doesn't mean you don't try."

"I didn't mean it that way. But, sometimes running is easier than staying."

"She's 13 and dumb. Someone gets her high and promises cash and a road trip to the Cities." Brody peers out the open window with hard eyes. "Next thing she knows she's in some God forsaken pit of a place with guys having their way with her."

The chainsaw's buzz is unrelenting.

"Maddy said Aimee's mom brought her home."

"After a detective found her." Brody's breath is high and fast in his broad chest. "Apparently, he was undercover in the house trying to make a drug bust. At least he had the decency to put her out back near the dumpster when she passed out. A real hero for sneaking her out and calling 911."

"Jesus."

"The prick probably joined in for all we know. Bastard, chicken shit."

"But he arrested the guys, right?"

"And ruin a perfectly good case over a drunk, high Native girl?"

Brody lowers his gaze and says softly. "She only stares at the wall. She doesn't even cry anymore."

Silence fills the space between us.

I remember Aimee standing alone outside the dance and Brody leaving to help her look for her sister. Her voice and eyes were hard, impenetrable and her words harsh. It felt personal. I had no idea what she was going through.

With narrowed eyes and a locked jaw, Brody says, "So help me God, if I find the son-of-a-bitch who took her there, I'll kill him."

My stomach feels queasy and my head pounds with the chainsaw's constant, high pitched buzz and all that Brody has shared.

"I'm sorry about Aimee's sister and about coming at you about Maddy," I say. "She's really my only friend here."

A twinkle replaces the hardness in his eyes. His hand takes mine. "You're really pretty dense," he says, leaning in to kiss me.

The kissing starts softly, then becomes more urgent. I'm not thinking about what I should do or how long I have to do it, like I did with Dirk. I melt into Brody's arms, which feel strangely familiar and foreign at the same time.

Val offers me a ride home after we finish painting. She says she has things she wants to discuss with Mom. Even though I don't buy her clairvoyance crap, I'm not about to test it in case she picked up on something between Brody and me.

When we arrive, Zinnia is curled up on the couch engrossed in a movie. Mom and Val head into the kitchen and I waste no time retreating to my bedroom. Despite the time that we've lived in Raven Creek, cardboard boxes sealed with clear tape remain stacked against the wall near the small closet by the door. A sheet covers the window overlooking the street.

I kick a path through the discarded, dirty clothes. Bending down, my hands search beneath the bed. I begin to worry it's been discovered. But, my hands soon grasp and retrieve the bottle of Jim Beam. I unscrew the cap and take a long drink. The warmth in my throat spreads throughout my body.

Closing my eyes, I imagine myself with Brody: his strong arms embracing me, his soft lips kissing my lips and neck, and his sweet body odor arousing my senses like an expensive cologne. Time feels suspended. My body sways, tingles and pulses. I can't stop smiling.

"That looks good. Got more? I sure could use it."

I blink my eyes open. My smile disappears. Maddy is standing in the doorway. "Your sister let me in."

At first I'm speechless. Then, I stammer, "Why are you here?"

Maddy looks offended. "Can't your best friend come by to say hi?"

The only time she was at my house was when we made cookies before Christmas. Many times she suggested coming to my house, but each time I found a reason for why that wouldn't work.

"I'm just surprised," I say.

"Well, you wouldn't be if you looked at your phone. I sent you a thousand messages."

"My battery died," I lie, leaning over and returning the bottle to its hiding place under the bed.

Maddy crosses to the unmade bed and plops down next to me. The box spring squeaks as she adjusts the two flat pillows and reclines against the bare, colorless wall.

"This is cute," she says, holding Mr. Hoppy. "I used to have a Build-A-Bear with a pink tutu that I made when I had my 8th birthday party at the Mall of America. It got so ratty my Mom threw it away."

Downstairs, I can hear Val telling Mom that she'll check back next week. Then, the front door slams behind her.

Maddy sighs deeply and strokes Mr. Hoppy's silky, dirty ear. Drama is always her go-to. I can tell she's waiting for me to probe. Finally, she says, "Brody sent me a text saying he just wants to be friends. I think he likes someone else."

It's as if my brain has short-circuited. My mouth and lips are dry. No words form. My heart races.

"He denies liking Aimee again, but I don't believe him." Thankfully, Maddy doesn't wait for my muteness to subside. She groans, "God, why doesn't he like me?"

I plant my most bewildered look on my face and shake my head as if to assure her I can't possibly think of any reason why he shouldn't like her over anyone else.

Maddy reaches out and touches my arm. "Please talk to him for me," she pleads. "I trust you more than anyone else."

Thirty-Two

I TROMP DOWNSTAIRS Sunday morning unable to shake a dream. In it, Brody and Maddy are making out as I pound on thick-plated glass, which separates me from them, and rain cascades over my shivering body.

In the kitchen, Mom makes breakfast as the sun beams through the window.

"Hey, sweetheart," she says. "The pancakes and bacon will be ready soon." Shimmering pink eyeshadow and mascara highlight her large blue eyes. Blush dusts her cheeks and gloss coats her lips. She's dressed in black jeans and a loose shirt. Her hair is blown out.

I plop into the chair. "Did aliens abduct my mother?"

She laughs. "Val set up an interview for a hostess position at the casino. She knows the HR director." Gliding two golden pancakes onto a plate, she hands it to me. "It's only minimum wage to start, but they have good dental and health benefits and even daycare for Zinnia when she's not in school."

Mom joins me at the table with the platter of pancakes and crispy bacon. "You and Zinnia are coming along because we're going to the mall in Bemidji after the interview," she says. "I'm cleaning out that little room at the end of the hall by my room where we've been storing boxes. It won't hold much more than a single bed, but we can make it cute for Zinnia. We'll get new bedding for both of you today."

I smear butter on the fluffy pancakes and drench them

with maple syrup. "I thought the baby was going to sleep there." I shove a bacon strip into my mouth.

Mom stares at the creamed coffee in the stainless steel travel mug.

"You okay?"

"I had a miscarriage last week," she says.

"Why didn't you tell me?"

"I thought the bleeding was normal," she says, using her napkin to wipe away a tear. "But it didn't stop and there was no heartbeat when Val took me to the doctor."

I reach for her trembling hand. "I'm sorry."

She strokes my cheek with her free hand and says, "At least I have you and Zinnia."

Zinnia and I wait in the car while Mom goes into the casino for the job interview. Zinnia sleeps in back while I text Brody about walking when we return from shopping.

A sharp rap on the passenger window startles me. Jags peers in. He motions for me to lower the window, which I reluctantly do, but only a crack.

The last time I saw Jags was at the courthouse when Dad decided to take the plea bargain. In the six weeks that followed, and before Dad took off, I overheard fights about the amount of time Dad was spending with Jags and his trips that lasted days with no explanation.

"Hey, doll, what ya doing here?"

"Mom has a job interview."

Jags glances into the backseat. "I bet you were cute too when you were her age." He smells like cigarettes and stale beer.

"You don't have to talk to me. I know how busy you are."

The sarcasm eludes Jags. He takes out a pack of Marlboro's from the front pocket of his faded jean jacket. "I'm never too busy for you, sweet thing."

My finger lingers on the button controlling the window.

"See you got yourself a boyfriend," he says, putting a cigarette in the corner of his tilted mouth. He flicks the lighter without shifting his narrow eyes off me. After taking a slow, long drag, he releases smoke out the side of his crooked mouth into the air.

"I don't know what you're talking about," I say.

"Don't tell me you kiss guys who aren't your boyfriend?"

How would Jags know about Brody and me?

"What would your dad think about you kissing Dirk, let alone going to a dance with him?" His eyes lock with mine. "I can't imagine he'd be happy about that, would he?"

"Oh, well, we broke up."

Jags bites the corner of his mouth, seemingly unsure of my declaration. "Did he take it hard?"

"No. It was pretty much mutual."

He looks unconvinced. "That right?"

My phone vibrates. Quickly, I tuck the phone face-down under my thigh and glance toward the casino's entrance. The sky darkens in the west. There's no sign of Mom coming out, only a hunched elderly man with a walker.

Jags removes his cap and runs his hands through his thinning hair before returning it to his head. White dandruff dusts his jacket. "I told your dad I'd help out if you ever needed it." His wink turns my stomach.

"You talk to my dad?"

"Nah."

Skepticism crosses my face.

Jags dramatically sweeps his arms down, then across his chest, and says with an innocent expression on his weathered, unshaven face, "Cross my heart, I don't know what happened to him or where he is."

"Whatever. He could be dead for all I care," I say, shutting the window and turning away.

Thirty-Three

A HORN SOUNDS OUT FRONT as Mom and Zinnia sit on the living room floor and pour over the newly purchased items from our Walmart shopping spree. You would think Mom won the lottery rather than land a full-time minimum wage job. She overfilled the cart with groceries, an inflatable mattress for Zinnia, and bedding for our separate bedrooms. Zinnia's over the moon about the rainbow bedding set and the plush unicorn.

"Maddy's here," I say. "She needs to talk so we're going on a walk and then having dinner at her house."

Mom doesn't glance out the front window to verify. Even if she did, she doesn't know Maddy doesn't drive a truck.

Brody pecks my cheek when I climb into the passenger seat. We make small talk as he drives and I leave my hand on the seat on the off-chance he might pick it up. His hands hold the steering wheel, oblivious to my invitation.

We don't drive long before Brody pulls over and parks near large spruce trees close to the train tracks on the edge of town. The March sun feels warm on my face despite the temperatures hovering in the low 40's.

As we walk on the mostly clear tracks, Brody talks about the fishing opener in early May, still nearly six weeks away. When I can no longer feign interest, I change the subject. "You excited to graduate?"

He shrugs. "It's better than not."

"I hear you're doing National Guard while going to Bemidji State."

"They got a decent bass fishing team."

"You're fishing in school?"

"Yeah, some guys I know made it to the National Collegiate Bass Fishing tournament in Alabama. It was televised and everything. A buddy of mine who went to Stevens Point-Wisconsin even won a bad ass boat in a tournament and is going pro."

"What about football? Weren't you up for a scholarship?"

"Too many concussions. There's not a lot of physical contact in fishing. And, I'm into having fun." He takes my hand. "Just so you know, I asked Val if I could come over when she said she was having you paint the back room." His fingers caress mine.

Our hands sway free and light.

Crows squawk overhead and the sun dips behind the clouds. A black lab with a graying snout barks and runs toward us with its tail wagging.

"Hey, girl," Brody says, bending down and rubbing her thick neck. She licks his face, then follows us. Even when Brody stops and tells her to go home, she remains at his heel.

Dirk emerges from the trees wearing a baseball cap, ratty sweatshirt and low-hanging jeans. He yells for "Lucy." When he sees us, his face puckers and he quickens his pace toward us.

He yanks the dog's collar. "You can keep your hands off my dog even if you can't keep them off my girlfriend." He then adds with a sneer, "Ex-girlfriend."

Brody grasps my hand tighter.

Dirk takes a step forward. "You think you can take whatever you want?"

"Maybe you should go back to your little posse of losers who actually think you're hot shit."

Dirk jabs his finger into Brody's chest. "Want to make me?"

Brody swipes Dirk's hand away. "Fuck off, Dirk."

Dirk swings at Brody, who ducks, releases my hand, and hooks his foot around Dirk's leg. Dirk falls squarely on a weathered railroad tie and moans.

Brody hovers over Dirk with clenched fists. Breathing hard, he says, "You never know when to keep your mouth shut, do you?"

Dirk scrambles to his feet and charges toward Brody. I wedge between them. Dirk elbows the side of my head. Pain sears my ear. I stagger forward, then fall to my knees.

Brody twists Dirk's arms behind his back. "You mother fucker."

My head throbs, but I manage to stand. "Don't. Please."

Brody releases Dirk with a push. "Get out of here before I kick your ass."

They eye each other with contempt.

"She's not worth my spit," Dirk says, wiping dirt from his hands. He whistles for Lucy and then retreats with his middle finger extended toward the sky.

I hunch over, my hands resting on my knees, which feel wobbly. My ear rings.

"You okay, babe?"

Babe? No one has ever called me that. Brody's arms engulf my shaking body. I melt into his expansive chest. His stubbled cheek presses against mine. He apologizes repeatedly, kissing my cheek each time. When he suggests going to his house, just for a while to make sure I'm okay before returning home, I don't argue. I lean into him as we walk toward his truck.

It's dark downstairs when I arrive home. Mom's in bed awake and scrolling through her phone. Zinnia is nestled beside her with Mr. Hoppy and the new Unicorn buddy in her arms. I sit on the edge of the bed, expecting Mom to ask about my time with Maddy. Instead, she glares at me.

"What's wrong?"

"I want to trust you," she says, not even trying to whisper. "Because I have a lot of things to worry about right now and I can't have one of them being you. I need you to stay out of trouble and make good decisions."

"I do," I say indignantly.

"Really?"

"Yes."

"You're not drinking?"

I throw up my hands. "Why are you drilling me? I'm a little late. I'm sorry. I should have texted you I'd be late, but I didn't think it was that big of a deal since I said I'd be back after dinner."

"I'm worried about you drinking."

"My head hurts and I have to study."

When I start to rise, Mom says, raising her voice. "You're not going anywhere. We're having this conversation. Now."

"Fine. Have I drank before? Yes. Am I a big partier? No. I hate the taste of beer. It makes me sick. I get good grades, work, and do everything around here, if you haven't noticed. I don't appreciate the third-degree."

"I don't care if you appreciate it or not. You are not going to turn out like your dad. Not if I can help it."

A slap would have been worse.

"What's that supposed to mean?"

"The drinking."

"I said I don't go to parties."

"Bri, it scares the hell out of me to find an empty bottle of Jim Beam under your bed." Zinnia stirs and Mom strokes her hair while staring at me. "Drinking alone? It scares me. I never expected this of you."

She reaches for my hand, which I snatch from her reach.

Mom sighs, her eyes sad. It's clear that she's been crying.

"There wasn't a time when your dad and I went out that he didn't drink. After we got married, I found bottles of alcohol hidden in lots of places, including under the bed and in his closet. He'd get mad if I asked him not to drink." Mom removes a strand of Zinnia's hair from her flushed face. She says, "I tried being perfect so he wouldn't need to drink. I felt I was the reason he drank. He said it was. So, it scares me to find a bottle under your bed when I'm putting on the new sheets and trying to fix up your room."

"You're making too big of a deal about this."

"What else don't I know?" Her eyes demand a response.

"I'm tired and have a lot of homework. Can we be done now?"

"I worry you will become like your dad and I can't live with that."

Thirty-Four

ON MONDAY, MADDY ARRIVES LATE to class and sits as far away from me as possible near the door. She refuses to look at me the entire time and leaves after class quickly without a backward glance. At lunchtime, I wait for her, as I do every day, but she never shows. There's no sign of her after school either. When I scan the parking lot, her car is already gone.

Despite the hundred texts I've sent her, Maddy refuses to respond. My calls go straight to voicemail.

Brody says we need to come clean with Maddy, especially after Dirk saw us, but I can't if she avoids me.

I decide to walk to her house before going home. The drizzle that started at the beginning of my walk thickens to fat raindrops.

Maddy's car is parked in the driveway when I approach the sprawling brick split-level house with the wood rail corner fence. Red-capped gnomes sit among white rocks. The front oak door's thick decorative glass doesn't allow me to see inside. Despite Skipper's relentless barking when I ring the bell, no one answers.

I'm about to leave when Maddy opens the door slightly. "Why are you here?"

"We need to talk."

"There's nothing to talk about," she says, "I can't believe I was so stupid to think we were friends."

"We are friends."

Maddy blocks Skipper from greeting me. "Dirk saw you and Brody."

"We were just talking. It was no big deal."

"That's not what Dirk said."

Wind slaps my face. "He hates me and would say anything to turn you against me."

"You want Brody."

"Seriously? You always beg me to talk to Brody, but when I do, you want to disown me?"

Maddy's eyes me skeptically. "You were talking about me?"

I tell myself that it would only hurt Maddy if she knew the truth about Brody and me.

"Yeah. You know guys don't know what they want. He's confused. I just listened. That's all. Dirk doesn't know shit."

Doubt is etched between Maddy's eyebrows. "He said you were holding hands."

"Don't you think he'd say anything to get you to hate me and Brody? He came at Brody and wanted to beat him up. I tried to stop it. See?" I turn my face so she can view the bruise by my ear. "Honestly, Maddy," I say, "The whole time we talked about you. There's nothing between us. I promise."

Maddy's sad eyes finally soften with relief and hope. My gut wrenches. Unlike lies that spring from necessity, this one is born of cowardice.

Thirty-Five

I'VE NOT TOLD ANYONE, including Maddy or Brody, that April Fools' Day marks my 17th birthday. Mom, giddy all week, insists I come home right after work today as she's making my favorite meal: baked chicken, cheesy rice, green bean casserole and, of course, red velvet cake.

The aroma of those flavors greets me when I open the front door.

"Hello," I call out.

"In here," Mom replies.

My stomach grumbles as I walk toward the kitchen. When I push the door open, Mom, Zinnia, Val and Maddy shout, "Surprise!"

Yellow streamers taped to the ceiling hang almost to the ground near the kitchen's entrance. I sweep aside the streamers like the beads at work.

I never expected a party.

Zinnia runs and jumps into my arms. She thrusts forward a card she drew with colored markers. "It's you!" The image resembles a snowman with short brown hair and a long, pointy nose. Eagerly, she asks, "Do you like it?"

I kiss her cheek. "It's the best ever." She beams and clings to my neck.

Mom envelopes us in a three-way hug. "How can I be old enough to have a 17-year-old?"

Most people would never guess Mom is nearly 35. She looks barely old enough to buy alcohol and usually is carded (as she always boasts).

A timer goes off, which breaks the huddle.

Val, sitting at the table with a colorful woven shawl draped over her shoulders, motions me over. Her weathered, deeply lined skin hangs on her thinning face. Most days now she's too tired to work more than a few hours. Carrying Zinnia, I go and sit down. The two-layer red velvet cake with cream cheese frosting serves as the table's centerpiece.

Maddy sits beside Val. She's wearing gold hoop earrings and a short waisted lilac colored sweater that highlights her narrow waist. She hands me a small package. "I knew the minute I saw this that I had to get it for you. Open it."

"Go ahead," Mom, says. "The party's officially started."

I untie the pink satin ribbon, which Zinnia quickly claims, and rip the shiny paper off to reveal a square black box. Inside, atop white cotton, is a silver bracelet with the engraved inscription: Not sisters by blood, but sisters by heart.

Maddy looks at me eagerly. "Do you like it?"

"It's beautiful." I slip the smooth, thin bracelet on my wrist, bending the ends together to tighten it. "But, you shouldn't have spent so much."

Maddy holds her arm up, revealing a matching bracelet. "We're sister-friends forever."

Val kicks a "Happy Birthday" bag toward me. I lift the large bag from the floor and Zinnia promptly removes the purple tissue paper. Inside, there are at least twenty different bottles of acrylic paints, a plastic palette, seven different-sized paint brushes, acid-free Acrylic paper, and a book entitled, "A Beginner's Guide to Acrylic Painting."

"This is incredible, thank you."

"If the Great Spirit gives you talent, don't waste it." Val starts coughing, raw and persistent.

Pushing Zinnia off my lap, I grab the box of tissues on

the counter and a glass of water. Placing both before her, I rub her back and wait. When the coughing subsides, Val takes a sip of water and closes her eyes.

Mom looks concerned.

"She's okay," I say, even though the coughing fits have gotten longer and there's more blood in the discarded tissues.

"I don't need you all looking at me," Val barks. "All I need is a tall glass of brandy when I get home. So, keep this party moving."

The front doorbell rings and Mom leaves to answer it. While she's gone, Zinnia examines the bracelet and declares it fancy.

Brody enters the kitchen carrying a bouquet of red bud roses with white baby's breath. They are wrapped in green tissue paper and protected by clear cellophane.

"Happy birthday." Brody hands me the flowers and kisses my cheek.

Mom looks surprised.

"I invited Brody," Val declares, eliminating the confusion surrounding his unexpected appearance.

The look Maddy shoots Brody is similar to ones I've seen her give other guys she deems unworthy while the look she gives me is worse. It's comingled anger and hurt.

Mom, oblivious to the energy shift, announces she'll be right back with my present.

Zinnia scrambles onto my lap and her small hands cover my eyes. "Don't peek." Her breath is sweet from the frosting she's been stealing. She squirms as we wait for Mom's return.

"Okay. Open your eyes."

When I do, Mom is holding a brownish-black puppy wearing a "Happy Birthday" bandana. It's the size of a pop can.

Zinnia bounces with excitement. "What will we name her?"

"Him." Mom clarifies. "It's up to Bridget. He's her dog."

"You said we couldn't get a dog." I stroke the soft fur of the big bellied puppy with eyes like tiny black marbles.

"I think we're ready for one now," Mom says.

Ever since I was Zinnia's age, I begged for a dog. It didn't matter what kind. I had a soft-sided, thick book with pictures and information about all the different dog breeds. I'd pour over each picture, memorizing all the details, and name each dog. The worn book is packed in one of the boxes lining my bedroom wall.

Mom says, "I'm not sure what he is, maybe some kind of Shih Tzu-Terrier mix."

"Dogs are a lot of work and cost money." Val scowls. "And this one doesn't even look old enough to leave its ma's teat."

"My co-worker, Brad, was practically giving them away."

Val huffs. "What are you thinking adding more work to Bridget's plate?"

The puppy licks my face. "I'm going to call him Rascal," I announce, nuzzling my nose in his silky fur. I turn to Maddy. "Do you want to hold him?"

"No, I have to go."

"But, we haven't eaten or cut the cake," Mom says.

"I don't feel good all of a sudden." She bolts out of the kitchen.

I quickly hand Rascal to Mom, push Zinnia off my lap, and go after Maddy. "Wait. I can explain." I grab her arm to stop her from leaving. "I didn't tell you because I didn't want to hurt you."

Maddy removes my hand from her arm. "Well, you did. Enjoy your birthday."

Thirty-six

NOW THAT SCHOOL'S OUT, I don't have Maddy's cold silence as a daily reminder of what a shitty friend I was to her, but I wear the bracelet she gave me. Brody thinks Maddy's reaction is overblown, but I never told him the full story.

At work today, I receive a text from Val asking me to come over after work without Zinnia or Mom. Luckily, it's Mom's day off, so I'm free to go see Val after closing.

When I open Val's unlocked door, she's laying, eyes closed, on the moss colored couch facing the lake. Pine trees border the vast shore. The late afternoon sun glistens off the blue, still water. The multi-colored patchwork quilt, which was her mama's, is drawn to Val's chin. Her hair is unleashed and covering the white pillow.

Softly, I slip out of my shoes and cross the wood planked floor. Crouching, I lower my head toward Val's ashen face and watch for breath, twitching, anything. When the coughing starts, I'm grateful. I release my breath and stand, tucking the quilt closer to her thin body.

"I'm going to make you tea with milk," I say. It's her favorite drink besides thick black coffee and brandy. "Has Earl been by?"

Val's eyes open slightly, then close again. She licks her cracked lips and shakes her head slowly.

I stride to the kitchen. "You wouldn't believe the number of people who came in today. I think we might have paid for the new mini-fridge."

Val remains motionless and mute as I heat the water in the stainless steel electric kettle on the counter. I open the avocado colored fridge and scan its mostly empty shelves: the milk's sour, the tomato's mushy and the cheddar cheese is moldy. I toss the spoiled food in the compost bucket on the counter and dump the full carton of milk down the sink. The vegetable soup that Mom and I brought by a few days ago remains untouched so I take it out to reheat in the microwave for Val.

As I close the refrigerator, I stare at the sea of pictures dating back years. Most pictures include a hooked fish, shot deer or assembled family posing for a holiday photo. I had spent time looking at the pictures before, but I never noticed the photo Val took of me after she cut my hair.

The kettle whistles. I toss a teabag into the mug and bring it to the living room, setting it on the low coffee table with engrained, concentric circles.

I sit cross legged on the floor near Val's propped head and listen to her labored breathing as I stare at the expansive, unmowed lawn sloping toward the lake.

Val's coughing resumes. She strives to push herself up, but sinks back onto the pillow. It intensifies. She withdraws a tissue from the sleeve of her wool sweater and coughs into it. Blood soaks the tissue.

"You need to go to the doctor, Val. They can make you comfortable."

She dismisses me with the wave of her hand.

There's no use arguing with her. I've tried. It only makes her ornerier.

The sun dips behind a thick, heavy cloud. There are no birds at any of the half dozen empty feeders or squirrels foraging for seeds on the ground. Blackbirds flit through the darkening sky.

Val eventually breaks the silence. "Have you worked things out with Maddy yet?"

We've had this conversation, or some version of it, many times. Val's the only one who knows the whole story of what happened.

I shake my head. "She won't answer my texts."

"You shouldn't leave it this way." Val grasps my hand. She says, "If you don't got friends, you ain't got shit."

"I've done what I can," I protest.

"Try harder. Be bigger." Her dark eyes are penetrating. "You might need her someday and she might need you."

Lighting flashes. Thunder claps. Fat raindrops splat the window.

"Brody deserves to know," I say. "You're like his mom."

"Having you, Earl, and now your mom, know is bad enough. I'd rather be like a cat who goes off and dies alone."

"You do know that even though you can be the biggest pain in the ass, nobody's leaving you."

Her unexpected laugh triggers more coughing. Finally, it subsides.

Val looks at me. "Did you finish it?"

I nod, pulling out my phone. I bring up the picture I took of the painting Val asked me to paint for her. In it, a raven is perched on the low branches of a pine tree bordering a narrow, winding river. The sky is dusty pink. Mist hovers over the rippled water.

Val moves her face close to the screen and examines the picture of the painting.

I spent hours studying images of ravens and then sketching them. I used the large canvas she specifically purchased for this painting.

Finally, Val says softly, "The raven represents metamorphosis or transformation." She pauses and licks her dry lips.

"When I sobered up for the hundredth time, I was driving to nowhere on fumes when I came to Raven Creek. It was then I knew the spirits were guiding me home. To myself."

Coughing seizes her chest.

Val reaches for me. I hold her in my arms, rocking slightly. I realize that she no longer smells like flowers. With her breath rattling in her chest and unbathed, she smells stale. I stroke her hair and caress the slack skin on her arms. We fold into each other.

There's nothing more to say between us.

Thirty-seven

VAL DIED THAT NIGHT when she was alone. It was as she wanted.

There wasn't a funeral or memorial service. She didn't want anyone fussing over her. Earl's job, I found out, was to paddle Val's old wood canoe into the center of the lake that she overlooked every day and distribute her ashes on the water's surface.

It was as if she disappeared, just like she wanted.

Val never mentioned what was going to happen to the Bait and Thrift, and I wish now that I'd asked.

Using the key she gave me, I let myself into the store for one last visit to say goodbye.

Everything is in place: the half-finished pack of American Spirit cigarettes is on the shelf behind the counter with the Bic lighter; the flaming red nail polish is near the cash register along with the deck of casino cards she used for solitaire; and the palo santo wood for cleansing the negative energy is near the docking station. My painting of the raven hangs prominently on the large wall in back where Val and I spent countless hours together.

I can feel Val's presence.

I light the palo santo stick. The tip glows red. Blowing it out, the sweet smoke lofts and dissipates. Slowly, I begin moving the stick through the air like I'm waving a flag. I cleanse the bait shop, then move through the dangling beads into the back. Pausing, I dock my phone and select drumming music.

I begin moving the fragrant wood in slow, figure eight movements. At first, my body's rigid like the palo santo stick. Then, I let go. My eyes close and my hips sway to the music.

All of a sudden, Val's voice rings in my ears, telling me to quit feeling sorry for myself and stand on my own two feet, not depending on anyone else to make me happy or take care of me. My laugh mingles with tears. I can't escape her telling me what to do even after death.

My eyes land on the picture of the raven that I painted for Val. I take it off the wall, tuck it under my arm and leave.

Thirty-Eight

IT'S TIME TO MOVE ON. To what, I have no idea. I send a text to Maddy and apologize, fully owning up, and telling her how much her friendship means to me. Surprisingly, this time I get a response: "It's cool. I'm back with Evan. Maybe we can hang out sometime."

Maybe things aren't always permanent.

Tonight, Brody and I spoon on the couch watching the Minnesota Twins throttle the Milwaukee Brewers in baseball. Rascal snuggles close to us while Zinnia's asleep in her room. Brody comes over most days after his National Guard training at the Bemidji Armory now that Mom works evenings as a server at the casino.

Although the sun has long set, the drapes in the living room remain open. I fight sleep, especially as Brody holds me close and gently threads his fingers through my hair, pausing at times to gently kiss the nape of my neck.

Brody and I must have dozed off because we jump when Rascal pounces off the couch and barks at the door. I go to the window. A car is parked directly in front of the house with its lights on.

Brody joins me. "Your mom?"

"That's not her car."

The doorbell rings in rapid succession. Rascal's yapping is high and persistent. Before we reach the door, someone starts banging on it.

Brody puts his body in front of mine. He unlocks the

deadbolt and opens the door a crack.

It's Jags, blurry eyed and scruffy. He narrows his beady eyes at Brody and slurs, "Why are you here?"

"I was wondering the same thing about you."

Jags pushes past Brody and staggers toward me. "Hello, darling," he says with a crooked smile. "Did you miss me?"

"Hardly."

"I promised your old man I'd keep an eye on you," he says, his body struggling to remain upright. "Remember?"

"I can take care of myself."

Jags smirks. "I like feisty," he says, slurring his words and lurching at me.

In an instant, Brody has him in a head lock.

Jags groans. "Let go, man."

Brody, a foot taller and probably thirty pounds heavier, leads Jags, hunched over and swearing, toward the door. He thrusts Jags outside. "Stay the hell away from here," he yells, slamming the door shut.

Jags' string of profanity continues behind the wood door.

Brody, breathing hard, turns to me. "You okay?"

I nod but I'm shaking. He wraps his arms around me and we peek out from the side of the window. The passenger door is open. Jags, staggering toward the driver's seat, waves his arms and gestures toward the house. The passenger door closes as Jags slips into the car, which then guns away.

The light from the TV bounces off the walls, as the baseball game continues. It's dark outside. We watch, but no cars pass by the house.

"He's gone." Brody says.

I stare into the darkness. "Dad's back."

Rascal keeps jumping up on my leg, demanding my attention.

Brody's eyes widen. "You think that's who was in the car?"

I nod.

"Why wouldn't he come in?"

"He's waiting."

"For what?"

"Us. Being alone."

"Then, I'm not leaving."

I look up at Brody whose arms still hold me. "You can't be here all the time."

Maddy once asked me after they found Dad's empty truck if I was worried that something bad happened to him. Honestly, that never crossed my mind. Dad's left us before, always resurfacing when he's out of jail, sober, or back from some trip from who knows where. He always finds his way back into our lives.

Shortly, headlights approach. Mom's car pulls into the driveway and it looks like no one has followed her. Sauntering in, Mom's wearing her skinny jeans that no longer hang on her; instead, they highlight her perfect figure. She's traded her uniform top for a silky peach colored blouse.

"Your shift ended well over an hour ago," I say. "Where were you?"

"Sorry, honey, some of us went out for Char's birthday." She flings her purse onto the chair and sits down.

"You could have texted me."

"I know. I'm sorry. It was spontaneous." She eases her feet from strappy sandals.

A floral scarf tied around her neck slips down, revealing a hickey. Mom pulls the scarf up, avoiding my eyes.

"Dad give that to you?"

From the look on Mom's face, he didn't.

Thirty-Nine

MOM CALLS THE CASINO in the morning and reports she's sick and unable to come in for her shift. We're both afraid of her leaving the house.

We don't speak as we sit together in the living room where curtains block the morning sun. A white plastic pedestal fan oscillates, circulating the thick, stale air. Mom's bloodshot eyes stare at the dark brew in the mug which has a bold yellow sunflower on the front and a small chip on its rim. The house is quiet except for the muffled voices from the TV in Mom's bedroom, where Zinnia and Rascal hole up, and the humming of the neighbor's lawn mower.

The doorbell rings. Upstairs, Rascal barks. Mom hesitantly approaches the door and opens it slightly.

"Mrs. Reid?"

"Yes."

"Ma'am, I'm Stan Miles, an agent with the Bureau of Criminal Apprehension. I need to speak to you about your husband, Carter Reid."

Mom examines his badge. "He's not here," she says, her voice cracking slightly.

"It's important we talk."

Mom allows him inside.

Agent Miles is a towering man with a crewcut and a red-tinged mustache. If I passed him on the street, I'd think he worked at a bank or insurance agency with his dress shirt, khaki pants and thick-soled brown shoes.

He glances at me, then Mom. "We should speak privately, Mrs. Reid."

Mom directs Agent Miles to the chair and rejoins me on the couch. "This is my daughter, Bridget." Her trembling hand reaches for mine. "I'd like her to stay."

"That's your prerogative." He looks squarely at us. "We have reason to believe your husband has returned to the area. Has he made contact with you?"

"No. I've already told the police I don't know where Carter is."

He wipes beads of sweat from his scowling forehead. "We've been investigating him and another person, Al Jaegers."

I don't say that Jags was here last night or share my suspicion that Dad was with him.

Except for a sliver of sunlight crossing his face, Agent Miles remains in the shadows.

"We have credible evidence that your husband is involved in a sex trafficking operation," he says. "So, we need your help."

My hand goes numb from Mom's vice-grip. She sounds like she's hyperventilating.

Agent Miles sits forward. "I know this may come as a shock, but I need to ask you some questions." His thick arms rest on solid thighs. "Is your husband gone for periods of time without explanation? Perhaps to Minneapolis? Fargo?"

"His work takes him places, yes."

"Mr. Jaegers go with him?"

"Sometimes."

Agent Miles clicks his tongue against his teeth. "He has an expensive, new truck. But, I can't verify employment. How'd he pay for it?"

She starts crying. "I didn't ask."

I put my arm around her.

"Some traffickers base themselves in small towns and then do runs, especially between the Twin Cities and North Dakota. The oil pipeline brings crews, mostly men, who pay good money for things, including drugs and sex." Agent Miles sighs and the lines between his eyes deepen. "They prey on vulnerable women and girls, especially those with messed up homes, who run away, or have drug or alcohol dependency issues. They groom their targets, making big promises of a better life."

"But, he has daughters," Mom says softly.

"Traffickers have daughters. It's a business. A lucrative one. You'd be surprised how many girls, in small towns and on the reservation, simply disappear without a trace."

I remember Val saying, after Brody told me about Aimee's sister, that Native girls get targeted by gangs and other low lives because no one comes looking for them once they disappear.

Mom says, "I don't know anything about this."

Agent Miles rises, digs into his front pocket and holds out a card to both of us. "I hope you will reach out if he returns. You can call me or the local police."

Mom rises and takes his cards with a shaking hand. After he leaves, she secures the deadbolt and turns to me, pale-faced. "Pack what you can. We are leaving for Grandma Rita's."

We finish packing Mom's car and Brody's truck just before sunset. Zinnia's strapped in back next to Rascal. My white t-shirt sticks to my skin. Without a breeze, the unusually hot, humid weather is suffocating.

Mom kisses my cheek. "Promise me you'll stay at Brody's house tonight and drive down as soon as he's done with National Guard training. I'll call you when we get to Grandma's house."

I promise and then, with Brody by my side, wave as they drive away.

Forty

THE NEXT AFTERNOON rain pummels the truck's windshield as we drive out of Raven Creek. The wipers, beating fast, cannot keep up with the downpour. It's difficult to see even a car length ahead. About 15 miles from town, I remember the painting of the raven that I made for Val. I forgot to grab it at our house last night when we left for Brody's.

"We have to go back for the painting."

"You've got to be kidding. It's going to take us forever to get to Minneapolis in this rain," Brody says. "I can stop by when I get back and bring it down the next time I come to see you."

"Please. It will only take a second."

My sweet, imploring look works. Brody turns the truck around.

The house looks the same as the day we arrived. The curtains on the front window are drawn. The shutter on the upper left window of my parents' bedroom remains broken and unhinged and the exterior needs repainting.

I dart, head down, toward the house in the pouring rain. My hair, tank top and jean shorts are soaked as I mount the front steps.

When I go to take the key from its hiding place under the welcome mat, it's gone. Tentatively, I turn the knob. It's unlocked. Hot, sticky air hits me. Water drips from my clothes and hair onto the scuffed, wood floor. As I reach for the painting near the staircase's banister, I stop, my hand in mid-air.

There's snoring.

Looking into the living room, I see Dad sleeping on the couch. One arm shields his eyes while the other hangs limp near a half full bottle of Jim Beam on the floor. A pack of Marlboros and matches from the casino are on the coffee table. Dad groans, then rolls toward the back cushion. A handgun sticks out of the back waist band of his faded blue jeans.

My brain screams, "Run!" But, I can't. My body remains frozen. My head pounds and I can't breathe.

This is my chance.

Seeing no movement from Dad, I creep forward and pick up the Jim Beam bottle. I stop and listen. The snores are soft and low. Holding my breath, I twist open the cap and tip the bottle. Amber liquid seeps into the stained carpet. It's sweet and woodsy.

Dad remains still, unaware of what I'm doing.

I reach for the matches next to the pack of Marlboro's. Tearing out a match, I strike it on the strip. Nothing. I try another. This one catches. Holding the match, I stare into the dancing light for a moment, then crouch and lower the flame to the alcohol soaked carpet.

Dad has no clue. It's so easy. And permanent.

But, this isn't a dream. And, I am not like my dad.

I extinguish the match.

Slowly and silently, I back away. When I reach the hallway, I grab the painting and sprint out the door toward Brody's truck.

Panting, I quickly climb in and lock the door. I look back at the house to see if Dad's coming after me.

Brody looks puzzled. "Are you okay?"

My hands tremble as I pull out my phone and retrieve Agent Miles' card. It's safely hidden between the phone and its case. Thankfully, he answers.

"This is Bridget Reid." My voice quivers. "My dad has returned and is at our house." My heart races as I listen to him say law enforcement is on their way and that I should get somewhere safe immediately.

Brody, overhearing the conversation, turns the ignition, puts the truck in gear and floors it. On our way out of town, he blows through the one stoplight in Raven Creek.

I grip the painting I made for Val. Her voice speaks to me, telling me to be strong and never forget home is wherever I am and family is whoever loves you.

As we drive further south on the two-lane highway, the sun peaks out of the thinning clouds. I take Brody's hand and squeeze it. Tears streak my face, but I smile at him and the road ahead.

Resources

Physical and Sexual Violence

According to UN Women, the United Nations entity dedicated to gender equality and the empowerment of women, **one in three women** worldwide experience physical or sexual violence, mostly by an intimate partner. It deems violence against women and girls a human rights violation and asserts that the immediate and long-term physical, sexual, and mental consequences for women and girls can be devastating, including death. Violence negatively affects women's general well-being and prevents women from fully participating in society. It impacts their families, their community, and the country at large. It has tremendous costs. www.unwomen.org

Trafficking

The U.S. State department, in 2021, states on its website:

> *"Human trafficking victims can be of any age, race, ethnicity, sex, gender identity, sexual orientation, nationality, immigration status, cultural background, religion, socio-economic class, and education attainment level. In the United States, individuals vulnerable to human trafficking include children in the child welfare and juvenile justice systems, including foster care; runaway and homeless youth; unaccompanied foreign national*

children without lawful immigration status; individuals seeking asylum; American Indians and Alaska Natives, particularly women and girls; individuals with substance use issues; racial or ethnic minorities; migrant laborers, including undocumented workers and participants in visa programs for temporary workers; foreign national domestic workers in diplomatic households; persons with limited English proficiency; persons with disabilities; LGBT+ individuals; and victims of intimate partner violence or other forms of domestic violence."

https://www.state.gov/humantrafficking-about-human-trafficking/#victims

- **National Domestic Violence Hotline:**
  1-800-799-7233 (SAFE); 24/7 hotline that provides essential tools and support to help survivors of domestic violence. www.ndvh.org; https://www.thehotline.org

- **Childhelp National Child Abuse Hotline:**
  1-800-4-A-CHILD (1-800-422-4453); 24/7 confidential hotline with resources to aid every child abuse situation. https://childhelphotline.org

- **National Human Trafficking Hotline:**
  1-888-373-7888; 24/7 multilingual anti-trafficking hotline. https://humantraffickinghotline.org

- **StrongHearts Native Helpline:**
  1-844-7NATIVE (762-8483); 24/7 hotline that provides confidential and anonymous culturally-appropriate domestic, dating and sexual violence helpline for Native Americans. https://strongheartshelpline.org

- **National Runaway Safeline:**
  1-800-RUNAWAY or 1-800-786-2929; 24/7 hotline whose mission is to keep runaway, homeless and at-risk youth safe and off the street. https://www.1800runaway.org

acknowledgments

MY HUSBAND, DAVID GRAHAM, IS unwavering in his support and encouragement. No one has spent more hours listening to me talk about this book, which has been bubbling up for many years, and offering invaluable feedback. He's my greatest cheerleader and love. Our children, Andrew, Connor, and Kate, have given honest input on the book and helped keep it real. I'm blessed to be their mother.

Liz Christopherson, next to my husband, has spent more hours than I'll ever know reading the many drafts and making editing suggestions. No one is better than Liz in catching the inconsistencies and fine details. Also, she's a terrific sister.

Not only have the following generously given encouragement, support, and friendship to me over the years, they make the world a kinder, better place: Jeanne Cotter, Janet DesLauriers Morris, Don McNeil, Jessica Roe, Paula Baker, Char Mason, Judy Walker, Laura Liu, Myrna Marofsky, Shelley Carthens Watson, Pam French, Velma Korbel, Pam Axberg, Laura Braafladt, Mary Kero, Lisa Wolfe, Judy Cummings, Karl Reichert, Jean Sazevich, Kris Leuer Beatrez, Kathy Herzog Olson, Molly Dahl Grosse, Jan Mohrfeld, Susan King Christensen, Pat Hoven, Beth LaBreche, Sonia Cairns, Terrie Wheeler, and Terrie Shepherd.

A shout out to Bonnie Morris, Michael Robins and my friends at the Illusion Theater and School. Since 1974, the Illusion has been producing works and educational programs that are groundbreaking, empowering and transformational. Their fine work and enduring passion inspire me.

The Twin Cities is fortunate to have the Loft Literary Center. It is there that I first met Mary Carroll Moore. Over the many years, I've taken classes with Mary at the Loft and Madeline Island School of the Arts. I'm forever grateful for her honest feedback, suggestions and encouragement. She is the finest writing teacher and coach I've had the privilege of working with. I'm also grateful that Mary introduced me to Rachel Moulton, who helped edit the book. Also through the Loft, I took a class with agent Barbara Poelle and author Heather Herrman. They, and the writers in this class, helped shape the characters and story-line.

Sydney Miller, Danaeh Morris, and Margaret Dow provided valuable suggestions to improve the book.

My teachers and yoga buddies at Devanadi and Jeannine Ouellette and the writers at the Elephant Rock retreat inspired me to let go and play more, which is so important to the creative process.

Ryan Scheife at Mayfly Design, Autumn Lee, and Hilma Bonhiver provided their creative talents to this book and its launch.

Finally, my mom, Elizabeth Jane Pautz, encouraged me to use my voice to speak up. She always put my siblings and me first, her love always evident.

Made in the USA
Monee, IL
10 December 2021